Silhouette of a Sparrow

Also by Molly Beth Griffin
Loon Baby

Silhouette
of a
Sparrow

Molly Beth Griffin

milkweed
editions

© 2012, Text by Molly Beth Griffin

All rights reserved. Except for brief quotations in critical articles or reviews, no part of this book may be reproduced in any manner without prior written permission from the publisher: Milkweed Editions, 1011 Washington Avenue South, Suite 300, Minneapolis, Minnesota 55415.
(800) 520-6455
www.milkweed.org

Published 2012 by Milkweed Editions
Cover design by Gretchen Achilles, Wavetrap Design
Cover art by Elsa Mora
Author photo by Kevin Obsatz
Interior design by Ann Sudmeier
The text of this book is set in Weiss
12 13 14 15 16   5 4 3 2 1
First Edition

Manufactured in Canada in June 2012 by Friesens Corporation.

Milkweed Editions gratefully acknowledges the Dougherty Family Foundation for its generous support of our children's book program.

Please turn to the back of this book for a list of the sustaining funders of Milkweed Editions.

Library of Congress Cataloging-in-Publication Data

Griffin, Molly Beth.
    Silhouette of a sparrow / Molly Beth Griffin. — 1st ed.
        p.   cm.
    Summary: During the summer of 1926 in the lake resort town of Excelsior, Minnesota, sixteen-year-old Garnet, who dreams of indulging her passion for ornithology, is resigned to marrying a nice boy and settling into middle-class homemaking until she takes a liberating job in a hat shop and begins an intense, secret relationship with a daring and beautiful flapper.
    ISBN 978-1-57131-701-8 (hardcover : alk. paper) — ISBN 978-1-57131-704-9 (pbk. : alk. paper)
    [1. Feminism—Fiction. 2. Self-actualization (Psychology)—Fiction.
3. Lesbians—Fiction. 4. Ornithology—Fiction. 5. Excelsior
(Minn.)—History—20th century—Fiction.] I. Title.
    PZ7.G8813593Si 2012
    [Fic]—dc23

                                                                              2011036296

This book is printed on acid-free paper.

For Emer, of course.

SILHOUETTE OF A SPARROW

Safe upon the solid rock the ugly houses stand:
Come and see my shining palace built upon the sand!

—Edna St. Vincent Millay, 1921

Silhouette of a Sparrow

American Robin
(*Turdus migratorius*)

I was born blue. Life ripped me early from my safe place and thrust me into the world. It was all so astonishing that I forgot to breathe.

But the puffed-up robin that sang outside the window of the birthing room came early too, that March of 1910, and just in time. He flew north before the spring came so he could sing me into the world. His song said *Breathe child, this life was meant for you.* When I finally let out my first scream I flushed red as that robin—red: the color of life, blood, love, and fury. At that moment I earned my name, Garnet, after the deep red stone that's meant to bring courage. "Garnet, for courage," Aunt Rachel, the midwife, said to me, when I was just a squalling baby.

My mother gave me life that day, but I was the one who decided to take it. I claimed it for myself.

That's how the story goes. At least, that's the way Aunt

Rachel told it to me a hundred times over, even after I knew it by heart. That's the version I asked to hear again and again as a child, so I could wrap those pretty words around me like a familiar blanket and fall asleep thinking I knew exactly who I was.

Black-Capped Chickadee
(Poecile atricapilla)

It was the seventeenth of June, 1926, and the Thursday morning streetcar was four minutes late.

On the streetcar platform, tiny birds hopped and pecked around the feet of the waiting crowd. My eyes locked onto one bird, and as I took in the curve of its breast and the fringe of its tail feathers, my fingers worked with sewing scissors, snipping the image out of black paper. Faithfully, the chickadee recreated itself in my hands. A perfect silhouette.

The bird hopped too close to Mother's tapping foot, and with a startled ruffle of wings it hurried away. I tucked its paper twin into my pocket along with the scissors.

"Mind Mrs. Harrington," Mother said, frisking invisible dust from the collar of my dress. "And write us often." Mother fretted on my left, her nervous energy expressed in fidgets and little bursts of conversation like, "We can't have you getting polio, now can we?" and, "Oh, we will miss you, dear. Won't we miss her, Albert?"

Father brooded, still and silent as a ghost on my right. He gazed off across the tracks, probably reliving some painful memory of the Battle of the Argonne Forest for the thousandth time. He didn't need to speak and neither did I. Mother did it all for us, prattling on about polio, which was her far-flung excuse for sending me to the country for the summer to "take the lake air" with a wealthy distant relation and her daughter.

At sixteen, I was hardly at risk for polio, but the real reasons for my going were among the many things unsaid between the three of us as we waited for that streetcar. Mother needed time alone with Father, to try once more to bring him home from the war, and I knew it. I also knew that if I didn't go away for the summer I might end up engaged to Teddy Hopkins before I finished up with school. Finally, Mother's desire to expose me to the civilizing company of her husband's rich relations made transparent her concerns that I (like so many young people these days, as she'd say with a sigh) might stray from the path to true womanhood.

I'd given her no cause for alarm; years earlier I'd abandoned dissecting owl pellets and climbing trees to look into nests in favor of ladylike bird watching and silhouette cutting. Perhaps the modern woman had been liberated from corsets and granted the right to vote, but there were some things that still weren't done. I knew that, and she had no need to worry. But worry was what Mother did best, and there was no way to stop her.

Where *was* that streetcar?

Mother brushed off her skirt and pinned up a loose wisp of hair. Then she shifted her weight from left to right and back again. "Where could it be?" she fussed. "I hope it's not *too* late; I asked Mrs. Harrington to meet you at the station in Excelsior and she won't like to wait. The streetcar will drop you off right at the amusement park and it would be awfully confusing for you to find the hotel from there."

At last, as if conjured by those magical words *amusement park*, the streetcar swung into the station. Its rear doors creaked open and the crowd pressed toward the tracks.

Mother gripped my shoulders in her hands and kissed me on the forehead. Then she let go and nudged Father, still staring blankly ahead. "She's got to go, Albert." His name woke him from his trance and he bent to pick up my bags. He handed me the small trunk and the traveling case, and then his cold lips brushed my cheek.

"Good-bye, Daddy," I said. It was the right thing to say at that moment, but the words felt too heavy in my mouth, so I added, "Wish me luck."

He nodded once and a flicker of a smile passed across his pale face. "Good-bye, Gigi," he mumbled. Garnet Grace Richardson—Gigi. He so rarely used my little-girl nickname these days that the word flooded my mind with images of him tossing me in the air (*Fly, Gigi, fly!*), tugging my ponytail, suiting me up in his big rubber waders for a trek through the bog. Maybe Mother would be able to bring that man back to us—I couldn't help but hope.

I tightened my grip on my bags and pushed into the rush and jostle of the crowd.

Inside, the car buzzed with energy—full of families headed off to the amusement park for the weekend, and women and children going to the lake for the summer to escape the heat and crowds of the city. I dropped my token into the fare box and then the conductor, in his pressed uniform, took my suitcase and led me to an open seat. I slid down the bench toward the window and he placed the little trunk on the floor beside my feet. I settled my traveling case in my lap and watched through the window as Mother and Father walked down the platform with a foot of empty space between them. Soon they were out of sight and I let out a breath I didn't know I'd been holding.

In another moment, the car startled to life like a cat out of sleep, sending the women's ribbons fluttering in the breeze that came through the open front windows. I pressed my face against the glass as the city rushed by. Streets and houses flowed away like water down a drain and soon we were in open country, soaring like a hawk beside our shadow.

Hawk, I thought, and the memory swooped in on me out of nowhere.

"Mama, look what Daddy and I found!" The long, speckled feather arched out of my hand beautifully. "It was a northern harrier, a female, I'm sure of it! She caught a snake down at the marsh—flew off with it dangling from her talons. It was amazing."

"Garnet, do not track that mud into the house. Just look at your dress! What are we going to do with you? Albert, must you encourage her?"

I shook the memory away and reached into my pocket. I rubbed my thumb against the handle of the crane-shaped scissors for comfort. The bird's legs stood atop the thumb and finger holes, and its body arched up into handles. Its eye made the hinge and its sharp beak formed the blades. When Father went to war and Mother insisted I come in from the citified remnants of forest and field and start learning to be a lady, I began to cut silhouettes of the birds I could see from the window seat of my bedroom, from the front porch, from the backyard, and from the sidewalk on my trips to school and back. After Father had come home and failed to take up my side of the argument again, Mother showed her approval of this quaint Victorian pastime by buying me a special pair of scissors for my twelfth birthday. Or maybe she just didn't want me to dull my regular sewing scissors on the paper. No matter the reason for the gift, as the hobby turned into a passion, the delicate pair of scissors became my constant companion.

I pulled the chickadee cutout from my pocket and a nib of white chalk I kept wrapped in a handkerchief. The chalk was for marking patterns on cloth, but to me its purpose was to scrawl Latin names on the backs of silhouettes—names that, when I tacked the cutouts to the wall above my bed, remained hidden. I still remembered most of the Latin from the days when I pored over bird books in all of my spare time. Now that idle moments were spent helping Mother around the house and preparing needlework for my hope chest, I held onto this practice of scientific naming as a small rebellion—a secret whispered between me, the silhouettes, and my bedroom wall.

Poecile atricapilla.

I folded the chalk back into the handkerchief. My fingers itched.

Would there be hawks in Excelsior? Herons? Woodpeckers? I had to wonder. Would it be like our trips to Grandmother's farm when I was little, when pre war Daddy would take me out into the fields and the woods to look for foxholes and pheasant feathers? The flocks of sparrows and chickadees and pigeons above my bed cried out for variation that was hard to come by without venturing off the beaten track. *Maybe in the country*, I thought, *without Mother around for ten whole weeks . . .*

I stopped myself. What silliness. I was not a child anymore, and Mrs. Harrington would make sure I didn't forget it.

I pulled my embroidery hoop out of my traveling case and set to work. I was halfway through the *m* in *Bless Our Home* on the corner of a pillowcase. That trunk at the foot of my bed was almost full; my childhood was almost over.

Mother's education in the "feminine arts" encompassed more than just needlework. She'd taught me how to budget the housekeeping money, when to buy fresh produce and when to use canned, where to find the highest-quality fabrics at reasonable prices, and how to turn those fabrics into replicas of the premade dresses in department store windows. (Exact replicas, except that I always sewed mine with oversized pockets for carrying paper and scissors and chalk.) *We're not wealthy, Garnet*, Mother would always remind me. *We don't have servants to take care of these things for us and we can't afford to buy everything premade. You shouldn't expect to marry into that kind of life either. But with a little know-how you can live respectably and fashionably on a moderate income.* In just a few short years she'd turned me from a tousled little girl into a capable young woman with a hope chest full of linens and a mind full of thoughts of housekeeping and family life. If only I could ignore the fact that my heart was as heavy as that trunk, I might be happy.

Outside my window, the terrain grew wilder as we journeyed farther into the countryside.

When I finished the pillowcase, I looked over my embroidery. The letters stood up straight, but the pinwheel daisies around them drooped a little on one side. The overall effect was pretty good. I was admiring my handiwork when the streetcar lurched and braked suddenly. I fumbled my hoop and jabbed my needle into my finger.

With a little yelp I stuck the injured finger into my mouth. The metallic taste of blood hit my tongue and then was gone. Just a prick.

"Excelsior, end of the line," the conductor bellowed as the motorman brought the car to a screeching stop at the station. The passengers scurried to collect their things, jabbering excitedly. I stowed my embroidery, careful to keep my pricked finger off the fabric in case another drop of blood escaped, but then I kept my seat a moment and looked out the window while everyone bustled around me.

A fat woman dressed in head-to-toe Victorian whites stood on the platform, leaning on a silver-topped cane. A slender girl of about fourteen stood in the shadow of the woman's bulk, dripping in outdated lace. Behind them cowered a colored girl dressed in simple servant garb. I waited for the crowd to disembark, looking at the trio and beyond them—to the whiz and whir of the gigantic amusement park.

Oh, how it called to me! My heart skipped around in my chest for a moment as I gazed out at the glittering spectacle that dangled before my eyes. The tiny broken-down rides at the state fair in St. Paul had never held much appeal for me, so I hadn't expected the amusement park to draw me in this way. The bright, quick beauty of the place sparked a yearning in me—for what, exactly? *I will go,* I promised myself. *I must.*

Beyond the hubbub of the park the lake sparkled. The serene expanse of water calmed me, reined in my wild heart, slowed my breath. Finally, I retied the ribbons on my sun hat, rose from my seat, and collected my luggage. Clutching my bags in a firm grip, I marched down the aisle of the streetcar and descended the stairs, stepping into the heat of the day and the buttery smell of popcorn. It was time to meet my summer guardian.

Ruffed Grouse
(*Bonasa umbellus*)

She presided over the streetcar platform like a grouse stuffed into an albino peacock costume.

I opened my mouth to address her—

"You are Garnet, then?"

"Yes, ma'am," I said, dipping a quick curtsy that seemed expected of me.

"I am Mrs. Harrington, your father's cousin on his mother's side. This is my daughter, Hannah." At her name, the thin girl whose angular limbs seemed to be drowning in their lace and ribbons nodded her pointed chin to me in terse politeness. The haughtiness of the greeting made me dislike her immediately.

"Pleased to meet you, ma'am, miss."

"Take her bags up to the Galpin House and unpack them, Charlotte," Mrs. Harrington said to her maid. "Have the dresses pressed. We'll be up shortly." The young woman dropped a deep curtsy and took my trunk and traveling case. She paused a moment, her dark eyes laughing with obvious surprise and relief at the lightness of my luggage, and then hurried away. I would've preferred to unpack my own things, but I was not about to argue. Mrs. Harrington whipped open her fan and fluttered it at her damp face. "Dreadfully hot," she murmured.

"Have you already settled in, then?" I asked.

"Oh, yes. We take the train up from St. Louis the moment Hannah's tutor stops lessons for the summer." She said *tutor* with emphasis, and her meaning wasn't lost on me; Mrs. Harrington's exceptional children did not bother with something so common as a regular school—like the one I'd attended all my life. "Mr. Harrington and my boys care for the estate while we come up here and make our home at the Galpin in the summertime," she continued. "The summers are simply unbearable down there if you ask me. We've been coming up for years, since well before they built that horrid amusement park last spring and the riffraff started arriving. Shall we make our way up to the hotel now? I'm afraid it's a bit of a walk."

Without waiting for an answer she snapped her fan shut and set off at a leisurely waddle down the walkway. I stifled a giggle, thinking of the ruffed grouse as Hannah turned to follow and I started to do the same.

But then something caught my eye. "Mrs. Harrington, what is that enormous building?" I pointed to a huge structure off to my right as we moved in the opposite direction. Hannah shook her head as if to stop me from asking, but the question was already out.

Mrs. Harrington stopped abruptly and turned back to me. "That, my dear, is the dance hall," she said, biting the words off and brandishing her closed fan like a weapon. "That is where nice young ladies and gentlemen go to corrupt themselves with drink and dancing." And that was all she had to say on the subject.

The dance hall tugged at me as if by a strand of fishing line anchored beneath my ribs. Something in there seemed to be calling to me, and I was surprised to discover that I longed to go see what it was. I'd always been fascinated by the one near my house in Minneapolis, perhaps because it was off-limits and my best friend, Alice, was always scheming ways to get in. Mrs. Harrington moved off away from the offending structure and I had no choice but to follow. The dance hall, like the amusement park, would have to wait.

While we walked, I sized up Hannah. Although Father had visited these cousins a few times before the war, I had not met them. They came into the city briefly on one of their summer trips, but I was too young to remember the visit, and Hannah must've been a baby in the arms of her nurse then. Now, although she was younger than me and smaller than me, she tried hard to look grown-up. Not only had she dressed in expensive white lace, but she'd also twisted her hair back in an elaborate style that exactly matched her mother's. Or maybe her mother had done the dressing and the hair twisting, using her daughter as a turn-of-the-century doll. I couldn't help but dislike Hannah for her vanity and arrogance, but I pitied her too. She looked so uncomfortable in that outfit, and it didn't suit her a bit. *If I sewed her a proper dress*, I wondered, *a simpler one*, *a looser one, a sundress or a summer suit—would her mother let her wear it?* I doubted it, and I was sure the offer would offend them both. The Harringtons may have been family, but our families were far from close. They didn't even know about Father's condition. I needed to tread carefully.

With no idea how to befriend such a companion as Hannah Harrington (and little desire to try), I walked in silence beside her and kept a bit of distance between us. She cast her eyes down. Mine took in the sights as Mrs. Harrington led the walking tour.

"This is the entrance to the amusement park," she said, her voice betraying an edge of malice as she gestured to the arched gates. The park swelled with joyous shouting and threatened to burst out of its fence. *Later,* I thought. *Later.* I tore my gaze away and hurried along in the fat woman's wake.

Mrs. Harrington lumbered down a path that led us past the park and around the western shore of the bay.

"The docks are here," she said, "but the grand old steamers don't run anymore thanks to this silly new obsession with speedboats. A few of the smaller steamers, the streetcar boats, still make tours of the lake. We do enjoy a ride on the *Minnehaha* now and then, don't we, Hannah?" The pile of ribbons nodded her answer. "Perhaps we'll take you on it, Garnet."

"Yes, I'd like that," I said, imagining myself in the midst of an expanse of water—a fresh lake breeze against my face and the swell of the waves rocking me.

A strip of grass and trees ran along the western shore in front of us. "What's up there?" I asked.

"They call this park the Commons, after the Boston Commons. It's all public land. I'd like to build a little summerhouse in that cove up there, but the city won't sell. Pity. We're buying in Florida instead. That's the new promised land, you know, and it's very reasonable to buy at the moment. There's wonderful money to be made in real estate, even when you buy on credit."

I narrowed my eyes critically, but then I felt Hannah's gaze on me and worked to change my expression to a neutral one until she looked away. Mother had often cautioned me against ever spending money I didn't have. I snuck a look at Hannah and wondered if she was dressed that way because her family was rich, or just because they wanted to look rich.

"In any case, there are public beaches up there and lots of pretty little inlets," Mrs. Harrington continued. "Nice clean, clear water—not like those dirty city lakes—perfectly safe for swimming if you're inclined that way and if you've brought a proper bathing costume. You don't want to seem indiscrete. So many of the young people these days . . ." Her voice trailed off for a moment. Clean, clear water. I could hardly wait to feel it cool against my skin.

"Off to our left here is the town proper," she continued, gesturing widely with her fan. "Lovely little shops up there—all the necessities. It's very quaint, makes a pleasant stroll. Ah, we're nearly there." She nodded toward a gleaming white building up ahead, set back from the park on a bit of a hill and across a narrow street, overlooking the lake.

"Oh, it's perfect," I said. A grand double-wide staircase led up to a veranda that stretched the length of the building. Two more stories rested above the first, with windows looking east, over the Commons and the bay.

At last we reached the front steps. They rose gently, not steeply like in a normal house, and it was easy to climb them with grace. A bellboy bowed to Mrs. Harrington and opened the main doors at the top. The lobby was large and richly carpeted, with a huge polished wooden counter for a front desk. An ornate radio stood in the corner with pretty little sofas and cushioned chairs clustered around it, their flowered upholstery clean and bright. Electric lamps nested on shiny end tables next to glossy copies of *Ladies' Home Journal* and the daily paper.

Mrs. Harrington led the way to our suite on the second floor. We had a modern bathroom, a small sitting room, and three bedrooms. Mrs. Harrington had already settled into the large bedroom with the bay window in the very center of the building, and Hannah's little room nestled next to hers. Mrs. Harrington showed me to the tiny room in the northeast corner that looked out over the roof of the veranda toward the lake. It wasn't much but it was all mine, and I could tell after just half an hour with the Harringtons that the privacy it afforded would be a relief. The maid had already unpacked my things into the dresser drawers and the closet, and the empty luggage sat on the top shelf of the cupboard like it had always lived there.

"Meals are served in the dining room three times a day," Mrs. Harrington said as I pulled back the heavy drapes, opened the window wide, and looked out at the lake. "The dining room is on the south side of the first floor, off of the lobby. Hannah and I will be down on the veranda when you're ready to join us. We'll leave you now so you can settle in."

I stood there awhile at the east window. *Maybe I'll be able to see cranes fishing along the shoreline from here,* I thought. Then I pulled away to investigate the second window on the north wall of the building. It looked out on a huge silver maple tree. *And that must be a heaven for songbirds. I'll never, never close these drapes.*

"You have no modesty," I said aloud to myself in my mother's voice.

"I need to wake up to blue sky in the mornings," I replied in my own as I fastened the sashes firmly. "And you, Mother, are not here to chide me."

As my own words sunk in, I felt a great weight lifted from me. Without the confines of Mother's anxious hovering and Father's persistent gloominess pressing in on me, I felt light. I filled my lungs with fresh, country air and thought that there might in fact be some real health benefits to "taking the lake air" after all, even for me.

I left the window and searched for my sewing kit. The maid had tucked it into the top drawer of the dresser, next to my stockings. I fished out a pin and took the chickadee silhouette out of my pocket. I tacked the little bird carefully over my narrow bed—the beginning of a new flock. I resolved to look for a grouse in the underbrush by the lake as soon as I could get out for a walk, so I could cut its image in honor of Mrs. Harrington.

Then I changed into fresh stockings and made my way down to the veranda, ready for the Harringtons, ready for lunch, and ready for my glorious summer to begin.

Blue Jay
(*Cyanocitta cristata*)

"Will it ever let up?" I whined to no one in particular, tossing my needlework aside in a huff. Hannah went on crocheting a doily beside me as though my complaining embarrassed her.

"May I borrow your scissors?" Hannah asked. I handed over the plain ones from my sewing kit. She snipped the final bit of cotton on her perfect lacy round before passing them back. Her mother smiled proudly at the finished product and aimed a pointed glance in my direction. Hannah's work was always lovely—she finished projects quickly and seemed to enjoy every stitch. Her mother's glance said *You could learn something from my daughter,* and I couldn't deny that it was true. But I was tired of needlework, and Hannah's patience with it and her natural talent for it only made me irritable.

It had been raining for days. The perfect summer morning of my arrival showed me just enough of the beautiful lake town to build my excitement for walks amid exotic country wildlife, thrilling boat rides, swims in cool, clear water, and possibly even forbidden excursions to the amusement park and the dance hall. But dense clouds moved in just after lunch that day and a dreary rain began that was not to let up for a week. Between meals and naps, I spent those long days sitting on the hotel's veranda with the Harringtons reading magazines, quilting, cross-stitching, sipping iced tea, listening to the radio, chatting about nothing, and watching sheets of rain fall from the gray sky to the gray lake below. Hot, heavy air lay in a damp blanket over us all, and the stagnant humidity only made boredom more stifling and sleep more restless.

Mrs. Harrington rapped her cane on the floor and snapped her fan shut in a motion that meant *Waiter, bring me more tea*. I reluctantly picked up my discarded embroidery hoop. *Think of pink thread and even stitches. Think of Teddy*, I instructed myself, *not sky-blue jays and ruby-red cardinals*.

What was he doing right now? Helping in his father's office, probably. Or maybe running an errand for his mother—he'd take any excuse to drive the family car. Maybe he was making plans for a trip to the movies tonight with friends. With Alice—oh, how I suddenly missed Alice—and her beau, Adam.

Teddy and I had been going out together for almost a year. On Friday nights we'd go for burgers with Alice and Adam, and then to the pictures or the bowling alley or a baseball game. He opened doors for me and bought me milkshakes and let me wear his jacket when it got cold.

I was allowed to ride in Teddy's car if all four of us went, and it was more fun together anyway. I liked the feel of his arm around my shoulders—his pitching arm, strong and steady, squeezing me tight. Sometimes, when Alice slipped off with Adam for a while, I let Teddy kiss me. It wasn't magic, not like they say, but his lips were warm and it felt nice.

Before I knew what I was doing, I had snipped the pink thread and switched to blue. In no time the brown branches and pink crabapple blossoms in the corner of the handkerchief in my lap played host to a perched blue jay. My tiny reproduction of this large, sturdy songbird was unskilled at best, but he carried the sky on his wings and the color cheered me up in spite of myself.

The waiter cleared his throat; I looked up in surprise. He handed me a letter—a letter! A small neat envelope covered in curly writing that I'd know anywhere: Alice's. It was as if thinking of her had conjured the letter out of thin air. I thanked the waiter sincerely, thrilled to have a distraction, and tore into the envelope.

Dear Garnet,
Is it marvelous there at the lake or horrid with all this rain? I am thanking heaven that I finally found a job for the summer or I'd be bored senseless without you here. I'm just working in the ladies' department at Dayton's, but it's good fun. The other girls are a hoot and I get to try on all the new fashions. I even got my hair bobbed so I'd fit

in. I love it short, especially in this heat. Anyhow, Mother's all for the job, but Grandma just mutters about "shop girls in this family?" all the time. I know once I'm married I'll leave the money earning to Adam, but it's too good to pass up while I'm still single, you know? Ooo, Adam. He's been taking me driving a lot in his dad's new car. I keep putting the brakes on, if you know what I mean. I have a year of school left! But he's so gorgeous, it's hard to resist. We've gone to the pictures with Teddy a few times. He misses you a lot. But no one misses you like I do! Write soon.

Love, Alice

P.S. Have you been to the amusement park yet?

I read the letter three times and then stowed it securely in my pocket. But even without the paper in my hands, my mind kept turning the idea over and over: *a job*. That was it, the answer. With a job I could get out on my own, I could escape the Harringtons, I could *do* something. Maybe this inert existence was enough for Hannah, but I was going crazy. I needed real employment.

"From a friend?" Mrs. Harrington asked.

"Yes, a girlfriend at home."

She went back to her magazine and didn't ask more about it.

After another moment of stifling stillness, I'd had enough. I couldn't wait another minute. If I needed a job, I first needed permission to look for one, and that was where I had to start. I gathered my things, brushed bits of sky blue thread off my lap, and stood up.

"I'm going to my room," I said, "to write to Mother."

Double-Crested Cormorant
(Phalacrocorax auritus)

I went to sleep that night pleased with the letter I'd written. I reminded Mother that she herself had worked as a secretary during the war, and told her that Alice's mother had allowed Alice to get a job in a department store. I trusted that she'd ask Aunt Rachel for advice, and that advice would certainly be in my favor. So many young, unmarried women were working outside the home now that it seemed pretty old fashioned to resist the trend. I placed my faith in the belief that no modern woman could deny her daughter this opportunity, and though my mother was conservative, she was not so Victorian as the Harringtons. She prided herself on being fashionable—reading Freud and following scandals in the paper and hemming her skirts to just the right length. She would say yes. She had to. I put the letter into the hands of the bellboy, who would post it in the morning, and went to bed hopeful.

Three hours later I woke to an awful racket. The sound of steady rain that I'd gotten so used to sleeping with had changed to a clamor. Uneven cracks and thumps and thuds sounded outside my partly open window, and occasional muffled clunks came right into my room. I stumbled out of bed and over to the window. My toes burned with a shocking cold and I looked down.

Button-sized balls of ice lay on the carpet like sparrow eggs.

Hail.

I looked out. The dark sky had torn open completely and ice chunks thundered down to earth. They bounced off the roof of the veranda outside my window in syncopated rhythms. They littered the grass below. With faint sloshing they pelted the lake, and though I couldn't see it in the dark, an image of the bay popped into my head as an enormous glass of tea with ice bobbing from shore to shore.

The sound was deafening, but it was a relief to my ears after days of monotonous rain. I laughed and picked up an ice ball from the carpet. The cold burned my skin. I dropped the hailstone into my mouth and let it melt there, cool and clean and almost sweet.

Thunder crashed and a blinding flash of lightening followed just a moment later. The wind picked up to a fierce gale, and outside my north-facing window the maple tree swayed in the gusts. My joy turned to fear in a heartbeat. I slammed both windows shut and backed away from them, in case the hailstones blew into the glass.

Muffled sounds of alarm came through my door. The Harringtons were awake.

"Come, dear," said a voice at my door after a forceful knock. "We have to go down to the lobby now."

I threw a long dressing gown over my nightgown and slid my bare feet into shoes. I opened my door to find Mrs. Harrington and Hannah waiting for me, fully dressed but only half awake. "Come, it's dangerous up here," Mrs. Harrington said, ushering us out the door and down the stairs to the lobby like a mother hen.

The other guests, in varying degrees of undress, gathered in a hodgepodge around the front desk. The bellboy, fully awake and still neatly clothed in his clean uniform, was just addressing the group as we joined it. An air of panic circulated among the crowd, but the bellboy was calm. Professional. In charge. Stately and dignified as a cormorant, that large, dark water bird I'd seen on sandbars by the Mississippi.

"I'm going to lead you down the kitchen stairs and into the basement," he was saying. "It'll be safer there if the wind blows a tree over, or if this storm whips up a tornado. We've got some lanterns and candles to take in case the electric goes out. Grab one and follow me. Please be careful with the fire—these old buildings can catch so easily."

He set off for the kitchen and the group followed, picking up lit lanterns and candles from the desk on the way. Mrs. Harrington didn't budge.

"I'm not accustomed to taking orders from a colored

boy," she whispered to us, "and I'm certainly not spending the night in some dirty basement with servants. Who does he think I am? We're staying right here, thank you!"

Hannah and I looked at each other, alarmed.

Just then a rumble of thunder sounded that shook the foundation of the hotel. A window shattered somewhere upstairs. The lights flickered and the room blinked into darkness. The last of the lantern light disappeared into the kitchen.

All three of us bolted after the group.

The basement was hushed and dim and musty smelling. People sat on the dusty floor, huddled around the glow of lanterns and candelabras. Children curled into their mothers' laps and went back to sleep. I joined a circle of people around an old gas lamp. Somewhere a man with a deep and gentle voice sang a few verses of a hymn.

> *If, on a quiet sea, toward Heaven we calmly sail,*
> *With grateful hearts, O God, to Thee,*
> *We'll own the favoring gale,*
> *With grateful hearts, O God, to Thee,*
> *We'll own the favoring gale.*
>
> *But should the surges rise, and rest delay to come,*
> *Blest be the tempest, kind the storm,*
> *Which drives us nearer home,*
> *Blest be the tempest, kind the storm,*
> *Which drives us nearer home.*

Teach us, in every state, to make Thy will our own;
And when the joys of sense depart,
To live by faith alone,
And when the joys of sense depart,
To live by faith alone.

His voice eased the fear out of me and I dozed, leaning against a cobweb-covered wall. Mrs. Harrington and Hannah stood for a long time, not wishing to soil their clothes, but after an hour they gave up and sat. I was dimly aware of Hannah's hip touching mine—we were crowded together down there and the proximity was oddly comforting. Mrs. Harrington's quiet complaints drifted into my sleep and mixed with the words of the hymn that floated in my mind: *Blest be the tempest, kind the storm, which drives us nearer home.*

It was nearly dawn when the stately cormorant woke us with the news that the storm had ended and we could return to our rooms. Sleepily, we picked our way through the graying darkness, avoiding the glass and hailstones that littered the carpet. He, the bellboy who had watched over us all night, found us extra blankets in case a chill came into our rooms through broken windows, in case our blankets were wet with rain.

I don't remember walking into my room, or undressing, or getting into bed. Sleep took me before I found my pillow.

When I awoke, the sun was high in a bright blue sky. Disoriented, I took in first the tangle of my sheets, then the closed windows. I rose, meaning to open them—why were they shut? It was only when my toes found wet carpet that I remembered the storm. The panic. The danger. The way joy and adventure had turned to terror in an instant. I shivered.

I wrapped my dressing gown around me and tied the sash, then opened both windows wide and surveyed the damage.

The hail had melted in the sun, but the grass was strewn with tree branches and debris. Outside the north window, the maple tree looked haggard. Its leaves were tattered, torn to bits by the hail, and wounds on its bark showed that it had lost many small branches during the night. The sky had been scrubbed clean and now arched brilliantly overhead. The plants, though messy, were a lush green from all the rain, and the lake gleamed like it had never seen the sun before. The heaviness in the air had lifted and the breeze off the lake was almost cool. The morning felt new.

So did I.

The Harringtons, on the other hand, looked terrible. After lunch (which was our breakfast), they retired to their rooms to rest. The hotel was in disarray, with wet carpets and broken windows and a messy yard and no electricity, so it seemed like as good a time as any to get out of there. "I'm taking a walk," I said as the Harringtons headed off to their rooms. "I'll be back in time to wake you for supper."

Mrs. Harrington simply nodded and closed her door, too tired to spout opinions about the best walking paths or to caution me about places to avoid.

I tucked my new handkerchief into my pocket, silently thanking the blue jay I'd embroidered on it just the day before for his help in bringing the sky back—no matter his method of doing it. Then I set off out the door and down the front steps.

But where to go? *The park, of course.* My heart skipped with anticipation.

I followed the curve of the shoreline south toward the amusement park, but as soon as it was in sight, I knew something was wrong. The rides weren't running. The park was closed.

The storm. They must have repairs to do. I'll have to go another day.

Then I remembered my letter: the job! I didn't have permission to job hunt yet, but there was no harm in looking. I'd head off into town to have a peek at the local businesses. That way, when Mother's letter came in a few days, I'd be ready.

But first, a stroll along the shore. My heart greeted that wide expanse of lake like an old friend. This trip to the country felt suddenly like a homecoming, even though I was far from home.

As I approached the docks, I saw it. A proud, dark profile perched on a wooden post that stuck out of the water, a piece of a sunken dock. No, I wasn't imagining the bird, it was real: a double-crested cormorant. Just as calm and as stately as I'd remembered. My scissors flew without sense—as if *by faith alone.*

With the silhouette in my pocket and the hymn on my lips, I followed the road into town.

Ruby-Throated Hummingbird
(*Archilochus colubris*)

Mother's letter arrived four days after my stroll through the picturesque little town, four days after I'd wandered along the row of brick storefronts dreaming of what it might be like to work in one of the shops. I'd spent the days after that trip waiting and worrying and getting my hopes up and then forcing them down again. I was sure, one minute, that she'd send an enthusiastic "yes" and let me work anywhere I pleased. The next minute, I was positive she'd laugh at my request and I'd be spending the whole summer on needlepoint and small talk—even more confined than I would've been at home in the city under Mother's watchful eye.

But when the letter found me, sitting at supper in the dining room with the Harringtons, it contained both good news and bad. "I am glad to hear that the Galpin is comfortable and you are all settled in with the Harringtons," she wrote. "They are so generous for watching over you this summer." Next came news of Father, who she enthusiastically claimed was "on the mend." My heart soared at the idea that this summer experiment might actually help bring him back. Then Mother digressed into a recitation of mundane reports from home and passed along greetings from Aunt Rachel and Rachel's companion, Sarah. Then, finally, she addressed the job question:

> I'm sure you are anxious to know my decision on the topic of your letter, so I won't delay further. I have considered your suggestion of employment and I've decided I will allow it. It is important for a young woman with your amount of energy to remain occupied. I have written to Mrs. Harrington to ask her to find you some small job that suits your position and education. She has connections in the town there, and I trust she can set you up with something you will find enjoyable—perhaps you could be a companion to a child of a wealthy family. Any wages you earn can help with your room and board at the hotel, less a little bit of spending money if you wish.

Companion to a child of a wealthy family? Didn't she understand that I was already a companion to Hannah, and it was the utter boredom of her company that drove me to ask for a job in the first place? Oh, Mother! Always concerned about my pent-up "energy" driving me to unrespectable pastimes, always conjuring up tasks to keep me "occupied" and out of trouble. Well, sitting around with yet *another* stuck-up brat was not going to help. I slumped in my seat and pushed away my bowl of rabbit stew, tossing the letter on the table in a huff.

"Well, what kind of employment were you thinking of?" Mrs. Harrington asked after reading her own letter from Mother and seeing my less-than-veiled disappointment. "Did you have some better idea?"

I blushed, but I was determined to swallow my pride and give voice to my plan.

"I think I'd like to work in a shop." Mrs. Harrington's eyebrows went up, so I continued in a rush. "My friend Alice at home is working at a department store this summer and she enjoys it, so I took a stroll through town the other day and there were lots of lovely shops that seemed like nice places to work—the ladies' clothing store, the florist, even the grocer's—"

"Oh dear, not the grocer's," Mrs. Harrington cut in. Then she stopped to consider. Her face softened as she thought; first her mouth moved from its tight line, then her eyes relaxed out of their squint, then she spoke again. "Well, I would never allow Hannah to work as a shop girl, but actually it might suit you just fine." That was clearly an insult to my family's income and lifestyle, but if it made her sway in my favor, I didn't care much. I ignored Hannah's smirk and waited for Mrs. Harrington to go on. She stared over my head and thought a moment, sifting through notions in her mind. I bit my lip, drummed my fingers on the polished oak tabletop, waited.

"I know the woman who runs the hat shop in town," she said at last. "Charming little place, and Miss Maple, the proprietor, is a respectable enough woman. Perhaps she would benefit from your help this summer. The shop was a mess when I stopped by the other day. I will telephone your mother and persuade her and then speak to Miss Maple on your behalf."

This was kindness I'd never seen before in Mrs. Harrington, and it made me certain that her motives had more to do with being tired of my company than with wanting to secure my happiness. And clearly it would nourish her feelings of superiority to see me behind a shop counter; the idea seemed to please her in a perverse sort of way. None of that mattered to me in the least. "Thank you, ma'am," I said, finishing the conversation.

We ate a few bites in silence.

"Do you know if the park is still closed?" I asked, trying to sound casual.

"I heard somebody say they're taking the whole week to repair the storm damage and test everything for safety," Hannah said. "Could we go look, Mother, once it's open again?" The spark of enthusiasm in her voice surprised me.

"Oh, I suppose," Mrs. Harrington said. "There's no harm in a little candy floss and a ride on the Ferris wheel. Perhaps we could go out on the *Minnehaha*, dear."

The look on her face made it clear that this too was a concession. It would ensure that her charges saw the amusement park under her own supervision. Hannah would be safe from the "riffraff" while in her mother's care, and she could steer us clear of the more "vulgar" rides. Mrs. Harrington seemed to be full of compromises this evening.

Hannah beamed and a smile found my face as well.

But as much as I wanted to see the park, I'd hoped to go without the Harringtons—to see it on my own, without the snide commentary of Mrs. Harrington in my ear and without her rules guiding my every move. I'd have to keep my eye out for the opportunity to sneak away.

Once I had a job, I'd be freer to explore. Surely a job in the hat shop would be my summer's salvation.

Mother was not so easily convinced.

I heard the whole conversation because the only telephone in the hotel was in the lobby, and this meant that Mrs. Harrington was afforded no privacy for the call. Mother shouted into the receiver of our telephone at home; she was still not used to the device and much preferred to communicate via letters. But this was a matter of some urgency that required the phone, so I could hear her end of the conversation too, though faintly.

"Her heart is quite set on it, Irene," Mrs. Harrington was saying, "and I can personally vouch for Miss Maple. Loveliest career woman I've ever met. Proper and upstanding. The hats she sells couldn't be more elegant, customers so respectable . . ."

She mumbled something about "just a few flapper-types" before she could stop herself, but thankfully the comment was too quiet for Mother to hear it. I smothered a laugh in my hand.

Mother's voice scratched through the earpiece, saying something about "shop girl" and "disgrace," or it could have been "not her place."

The conversation went on like that for some time

before Mother finally succumbed. I couldn't hear her words through the earpiece, but Mrs. Harrington's smile declared her success loud and clear.

"Wonderful!" she proclaimed. "Don't you worry about a thing, Irene. I'll see that she gets settled. Oh, no trouble at all." She gestured to me, offering me the phone. I shook my head, not wanting to give Mother a chance to change her mind. "No, she can't talk now, Irene, but I'll give her your love. Yes, all right, good-bye."

With the earpiece safely in its cradle, I let out a squeal of happiness. I almost hugged Mrs. Harrington. Almost.

"We'll go to town in the morning, dear, and speak with Miss Maple. Time for me to retire now, I'm afraid. Do get to bed at a reasonable time, Garnet. You'll want to be fresh in the morning."

"Yes, ma'am," I said. "I will."

But before bed, I took a stroll down to the lake to collect my thoughts. The water shone pink from the just-set sun. The lights from the amusement park twinkled across the bay, but no shouts of fairgoers echoed over the lake. With the park closed, the evening air was still and quiet. It seemed that the lights were on just for me, a reminder that something waited for me there, in that park. I could feel it reach out across the bay and stir something in my gut. I'd go with the Harringtons, I decided, but I'd go by myself first. Somehow.

I turned and headed back up the hill.

In the hotel garden, a few lilies had bloomed since the storm. The unscathed blossoms matched the pink of the sunset and there, hovering above them, whirred a tiny ruby-throated hummingbird having a bedtime snack. I reached into my pocket to retrieve my crane scissors and quickly snipped its shape out of paper: the curve of its belly, the needle of its beak, the sleek plunge of its back. Then the bird darted away, but I held its image in my hands. The silhouette couldn't capture the brightness or the lively motion of that quick-winged jewel, but the likeness was there. This was no city-fattened chickadee. No. My summer flock would be different.

Maybe I would be different too.

I scrawled the Latin name on the back of the cutout and stashed it in my pocket along with the scissors and chalk. The sky had settled into twilight blue and it was time to go inside. I took the stairs two at a time and headed off to bed, eager for morning to come.

Snowy Egret
(*Egretta thula*)

Light poured onto my bed the next morning like warm honey. I lay there, feeling the heat on my closed eyelids, clinging to the last shreds of a dream.

A sharp knock jolted me awake, and Mrs. Harrington's voice came muffled through the door. "Wake up, Garnet. We should get there at opening time."

I mumbled something that meant, "Let me sleep," but then I realized what she'd said, where we were going, what today had in store. It was the thirtieth of June, and I, Garnet Grace Richardson, was about to become a career girl. I leapt out of bed.

Mrs. Harrington set a bowl of porridge on the table in the sitting room with a *plunk*. She must've asked the kitchen to send it up so we wouldn't have to wait for breakfast in the dining room. She was already dressed in her albino peacock outfit—her favorite togs—and a look of impatience had already settled onto her face. Clearly she was finished with her momentary lapse into generosity and indulgence. I hadn't expected it to last.

I made quick work of my breakfast and then hurried to dress, pulling on clean underclothes and stockings and a cornflower blue linen summer suit that looked nice with my eyes. I twisted my hair back under a smart blue hat that almost matched my dress and slid my feet into white shoes with low heels.

I checked my appearance in the washroom mirror. Mousy hair, freckled skin, lanky body. Just a girl trying to look like a woman. I sighed. At least I shared no family resemblance with the Harringtons. I had no round build or multiple chins. I had no pointy face or sharp-angled limbs. Even dressed in their finery, the pair of them made me feel positively beautiful. I'd actually never been so content with my plain looks and my simple clothing, girlishness aside.

But what would my new employer think?

"Come, Garnet. It's nearly eight," Mrs. Harrington grumbled from the sitting room.

I nodded to my reflection. "You'll have to do," I said in my mother's voice, and then I turned to leave.

"Is there a library in Excelsior?" I asked Mrs. Harrington as we bustled out the door and down to the lobby. I wasn't sure I'd spelled the hummingbird's Latin name correctly and I needed a bird book to check. In fact, I needed several bird books, I promptly decided. As many as a library might have. I kept one reference book at my window seat at home, but it had been years since I'd indulged in a stack of bird books from the library. Without Mother around to redirect me, I could linger over forestry records and biology journals to my heart's delight—but I needed a library.

"In the Sampson House, I believe. I'll point it out and you can stop on your way home this afternoon if you like." She was used to getting exactly what she wanted, and she was so confident in our plan that she assumed I'd be working today. My heart raced at the thought and my hands trembled a bit. My fingers slipped into my pocket and found my scissors, stopping to caress the familiar metal.

"Personally I never bother with books," Mrs. Harrington was saying. "I prefer the magazines and the newspapers, and that's enough reading for me. Hannah doesn't even care for those." She whipped her fan out as the bellboy opened the front door, her gesture ending the conversation, and then descended the stairs with an air of royalty.

Main Street smelled like baking bread. The town was warmer than the lakefront, but not hot yet, and everything looked fresh in the morning light. We passed the drugstore, the grocer's, the beauty shop, and the shoe store on our way to Miss Maple's hat shop. Finally, we arrived at a brick storefront with a pink, flowery, painted sign and a cascade of frilly hats in the window. It was such a tiny place that I'd overlooked it completely on my first excursion into town.

The chimes on the door jingled cheerfully to announce our presence, and a tired but genteel-looking woman called hello over her shoulder as she arranged hats with netting veils on a tall rack near the counter.

The shop was in chaotic disarray, as Mrs. Harrington

had said, but the hats were beautiful, like flocks of tropical birds roosting on wire trees. I set off down a row of wide-brimmed, flowery hats while Mrs. Harrington approached the petite woman and struck up a conversation. I peered at them through the hat jungle.

"Oh, a lifesaver you are," the woman was saying a moment later. Relief erased the creases around her eyes for a minute. "My last girl quit on me two weeks ago. Husband said she shouldn't have a job, said it made him look bad. Silliness." She shook her head, clucking, not catching the stern look on Mrs. Harrington's face or the fact that all three of her chins had dropped half an inch. "I've been trying to do it all on my own, but I'm afraid it's just too much during the summer months. I really could use the help. Just mornings, maybe. Come here, dear," Miss Maple called to me. I wove through the racks and approached the kind-faced woman.

"Garnet Richardson, ma'am," I said. She reached out and shook my hand warmly. I looked down, a blush creeping into my cheeks, while she sized me up. Did she see a confused girl who was trying too hard, or a composed and competent young woman? Maybe both. She nodded and reached for a pile of hats on the counter.

"When can you start?" she said. I looked up, shocked and relieved by her quick decision. She grinned at me. A pink hat fell from the pile in her hands.

I laughed. "How about now?" I bent to pick up the pink hat and straightened its veil. I placed it on the rack and turned it until it was just so.

"A lifesaver, a lifesaver," the woman sighed, hustling

off toward the back room. "I'll be with you in a moment and we can start your training today," she called over her shoulder.

"Well, that worked out nicely, yes?" Mrs. Harrington said. "I'll see you this afternoon, dear, back at the hotel. Have a lovely day." She gave a little amused chuckle and then waddled out the door. The chimes jingled, and I let out a long breath that deflated a whole lot of tension.

I looked around while I waited for Miss Maple to come out of the back room. I took off my own hat and put on a green bell-shaped one, and then turned to look at myself in a mounted mirror. I laughed at the young woman staring back at me, the hat making my attempt to look modern and fashionable and grown-up even more obvious. Too many mirrors today, I decided.

Miss Maple came up behind me, and before I could take the hat off she reached up and tilted it at a jaunty angle. "Perfect," she said. "It's a cloche hat, like the flappers wear. Like Clara Bow in the pictures." I looked nothing like the glamorous Clara Bow and we both knew it, not even with that beautiful hat on.

"No?" she said. "Not your style?"

"I've got too much hair." I took it off and put it back on its stand, thinking of Alice and her new bob.

"How about this one?" She reached for a wide-brimmed peach-colored hat with a beautiful white feather tucked into the band. She settled it on top of my hair.

"Is this . . . real?" I asked, reaching up to stroke the beautiful feather.

"Oh, yes, an egret feather, only the best," she said.

"Snowy egret," I murmured, my brow crinkling involuntarily. *Egretta thula. Poached,* I thought, recalling the Junior Audubon Society articles I read after Father set me up as a member. *That's illegal now, doesn't she know that? Killing all those gorgeous birds just to dress ladies' hats? It's not only illegal, it's appalling.*

"What's wrong, Garnet?" Miss Maple asked, seeing my troubled expression in the oval-shaped mirror.

"Nothing," I said quickly. "It's just a little old-fashioned for me, I think." Embarrassed, I returned the hat to the rack and moved away from the mirror, sick of looking at myself. I couldn't argue with my new boss about the crimes of the feather industry my first day on the job. Talk about starting off on the wrong foot. I grabbed my own hat and turned to face the confused Miss Maple.

"Where should I put this?"

"Oh, yours can go behind the counter. Then I'll show you around."

After that one awkward moment, my first day went smoothly. I learned about all the kinds of hats—how to wear them, who would wear them, where and when they should be worn—as well as how to take orders and wrap parcels and make change.

I'll like this job, I thought as I let myself out at noon and headed back toward the hotel. I tried to put the feathers out of my head—it would not do to oppose Miss Maple's business decisions. And who was I to worry about things like that anyway? I was no naturalist. I was no activist. I was just a girl with her first job walking alone on a beautiful summer's day, headed to the library for some decent reading material.

And I was going to be late for lunch if I didn't hurry.

Scarlet Tanager
(*Piranga olivacea*)

My first thought when she came through the door to the hat shop was *scarlet tanager*. It must have been the bright red lips that perched on her pale face. She had shiny black hair, bobbed, and dark eyes, and she wore a sundress cut above the knee and no stockings. Those lips! I'd seen just a few scarlet tanagers in my life—the first when I was ten and spending the summer with Grandmother on the farm in Iowa—and I'd always regarded that brilliant flash of red wings as a good omen.

The chimes jingled as the door closed behind her.

It was only my third day of work, and all the customers up till then had been older women like Mrs. Harrington, women looking for sunhats to replace ones blown away on boating trips and things like that. But this customer was different. Young. Beautiful. I watched her from behind the counter as she browsed the racks, and completely forgot about the receipts I'd been sorting.

"Do you have anything *new?*" she called from the same shelf of stylish hats I'd been so taken with on my first day. "I need something no one in this town has seen before."

"I don't know . . ." I said, scanning the shop with my eyes. I had no idea what was new. The whole section she was perusing was new to *me*. Miss Maple would know how to help this customer, but she had gone to the bank and I was alone in the shop.

The fashionable young woman sauntered up to the counter, one eyebrow cocked. "Hey, I don't know you," she said, looking at me steadily, "do I?"

She moved with grace, spoke with confidence.

"No," I answered. I looked down at the counter for a moment, feeling awkward under her self-assured gaze. "I'm Garnet Richardson. I'm just here for the summer."

I made myself look up and reach over the counter, and she slipped a slender, black-lace-gloved hand into mine. Up close I realized she was even younger than I thought. Older than me, but not by much. Eighteen, maybe.

"Isabella Strand," she replied. "I work at the dance hall. Have you been yet?"

"Oh, no, not yet. What do you do there?"

"Well, I dance," she laughed, and it reminded me of a birdsong. I couldn't remember which. It tickled my memory but I couldn't bring it to mind. *Probably something exotic,* I thought. "I dance with the big bands in the evenings," she said.

I blushed. It should have been obvious.

"So," she went on, "what do you think?"

"About . . . ?"

"A hat! Do you have anything new?"

"Oh, wait, yes. I think I've got just the thing." I rushed into the back room, stopping for a moment with my back to the door and trying to think where "just the thing" was. It had come in that morning with the new delivery and I had wondered who on earth would buy it. It was a red cloche with a sassy slouch to it and black ribbons sewn down one side. It was perfect. It was made for her. There—on the worktable where it had been unpacked and tagged with the morning's shipment. I frisked a little dust off the felt and scooped it up.

"Ta-da!" I said, pushing open the door and presenting the hat with a flourish over the counter.

"Oh!" she cried. "Stunning! Help me put it on." I moved around the counter to stand behind her and helped her pull it down over her slick black hair and settle it just so. She really *did* look like Clara Bow. The perfect flapper. Half the girls at school tried to look like this but none of them pulled it off like Isabella Strand.

"I love it!" she squealed, clapping her hands like a child at a birthday party, laughing that birdsong laugh I couldn't place. She spun around to plant a kiss on my cheek.

My skin warmed under her lips.

I scurried behind the counter to ring her up for the purchase.

"Will you come to my show? Tonight?" she asked after the money had changed hands.

"I don't know, I mean, I'm not really allowed."

"Your mother doesn't approve."

"No, though that's probably true as well. See, I'm staying with my . . . aunt, sort of. At the Galpin House. She *definitely* doesn't approve. I haven't even been to the park yet. I was hoping to sneak off soon."

"You haven't been? Well you must go immediately. It's opening again today, you know, and I'd take you myself this afternoon but I'm afraid I'll be in rehearsals for the new act. Booked solid. So you'll have to go by yourself."

I nodded. Today.

"And promise me you'll slip out some evening soon and catch my show?"

"Yes, of course, I'll try," I said. I wasn't sure how to accomplish it, but maybe it was possible. I wanted to see her again.

"Well, I will see you soon then, Garnet Richardson," she said with a wink, and then she was gone. Out the door with nothing but a jingle.

Within the hour I'd convinced myself that I'd imagined her. How could she be real? But whether the scarlet tanager existed or not, my convictions were stronger than ever. At noon, when I pinned my hat on and said good-bye to Miss Maple and pushed open the door, I set off with confident steps for the amusement park.

An hour, that's all it'll take, I thought. *No one will miss me for an hour.*

Ring-Billed Gull
(*Larus delawarensis*)

On Fridays the park didn't open until the afternoon, and that Friday, with the reopening, things were running just a little behind schedule. When I got there, after hurrying from work so as not to lose my nerve or waste too much time, the gates were still closed. The Ferris wheel towered over me, still but for the gentle rocking of the suspended seats in the breeze. The roller coaster track snaked overhead, empty of cars, and a huge spiderlike contraption lurked a little ways off, awaiting its first riders. The painted horses on the carousel stood frozen in midstride, waiting for permission to leap into life.

The park was nearly empty as I stood at the gate looking in, but the workers hurried around getting the rides ready for an afternoon rush. The crowd waiting with me was not large; the word that the park would be reopening today must not have been out yet. That was good news, since it meant the Harringtons would be less likely to know where I was when I didn't show up for lunch.

Behind the gates, the food carts were just yawning open their windows, and the sticky-sweet smells of cotton candy and caramel corn filled the air. I waited with the few other park-goers who milled around, watching for the gates to open and the rides to spring into action. I sat down on the grass beside the fence to wait, with only fleeting concern for the state of my dress.

A ring-billed gull perched on the fence post, eyeing the popcorn stand, and I snip-snipped his plump form out of paper to pass the time. He was no tanager, but he'd do for the moment.

Tanager. Isabella had been flitting in and out of my head in bright flashes of red all morning. By the time I'd arrived at the park I'd decided two things: she *was* real and I *would* see her again. The gull's image would be a gift for her. I imagined what she'd say when I gave it to her . . .

Is it really from your first trip to the park? It's amazing—you're amazing. Are you sure I can keep it? Then she'd squeeze my hand in hers and peck me on the cheek again. I wouldn't embarrass myself this time. I'd just say, *Of course you can keep it; I did it for you.*

The gull, the real one, took flight with a sudden flap of his wings and startled me back to reality. The park's gates were creaking open, inviting the visitors inside. It was time.

I rose, catching sight of a tiny grass stain on the skirt of my dress—would the Harringtons notice? Oh, I needed to be more careful. And I needed to be quick too. I pressed in with the little crowd that had gathered while I sat daydreaming on the lawn. Inside, the cart tenders and the ride operators called invitations to the first customers of the day.

"Catch a ride on the Mountain Railway!"

"Pack a picnic for the boat ride. Picnic food here!"

"Caterpillar, Caterpillar—hop on the Caterpillar!"

One by one, the rides lurched into motion. Everything slowly started turning, spinning, crawling with a few riders on board. Then it all picked up speed and the whole world was a-blur with twisting and rushing. Joyful cries rang out through the hot afternoon air.

My heart sped as the park came to life and I found myself running from ride to ride, giddy with the electricity in the air and the building heat. My blood whizzed through my veins like the speeding roller coaster and my eyes ricocheted from one attraction to the next, reckless as bumper cars.

Finally, in my crazed wandering, I stumbled upon a huge wooden tube that seemed to be rotating in place. No one was inside but the big hollow barrel spun anyway, a frightening challenge to every passerby.

"Come inside," the woman at the controls called.

"I . . . I didn't bring any money," I said, realizing my lack of foresight with both regret and relief. The woman paused, then shrugged.

"First ride's free," she said, and she gestured inside.

I swallowed hard and stepped up to the spinning barrel. I climbed the two steps and, with a deep breath to steady myself, set one foot inside. It lurched under me, but I forced myself to clamber all the way in.

The world shifted beneath me as I scrambled down the length of the tunnel. Inside the tube there was no up and no down, only dizziness and confusion. I stumbled and fell and the ground beneath my now-rumpled dress did not pause to catch me. It turned under me, and for a frantic moment I thought it would haul me all the way up its wall and toss me around until the operator had to drag me out, broken and dreadfully embarrassed.

Somehow I managed to regain my feet, though, and scurry unsteadily down the tunnel. Focusing on the still patch of grass at the other end, I tried to trust my feet to carry me. Without looking down, I tripped and tramped my way down the length of the twisting tube.

At last, I found myself back in the open air. I tumbled down the steps and fell to my knees on the grass. After a moment my jagged breath stilled, and I looked around me. The sky was up, the earth was down, and through all the spinning and rushing of the rides, the deep blue water of the lake stretched out with serene reassurance.

But somewhere beyond the lake was the city, and my house, and Mother and Father and Aunt Rachel and Sarah, and a part of myself that I'd left back home, safely tucked away at the window seat and in the hope chest.

Hope.

I hauled myself to my feet and dusted off the front of my dress. Then I let out a long sigh, wondering if I'd been hoping for the right things.

American White Pelican
(*Pelecanus erythrorhynchos*)

"And where on earth have *you* been, might I ask?"

I was praying that the Harringtons would still be in the dining room at their lunch when I got back, but I was not so lucky. Mrs. Harrington presided over the veranda from a wicker settee while her skinny daughter sat in a chair nearby with her ankles crossed and an embroidery hoop in her lap. Mrs. Harrington held her fan in one hand and an enormous glass of iced tea in the other. The glass was sweating and so was she.

I'd been away longer than I'd planned to be. I'd been missed.

"We expected you hours ago," she said, collapsing her fan and pointing it at me accusingly.

"Surely it's not *that* late," I said, flustered. "A big order came in and Miss Maple asked me to stay on a bit to help unpack it. I'm sure it won't become a regular thing."

This lying won't become a regular thing either, I told myself.

Hannah stared at the grass stain on my skirt and I quickly tried to cover it with my hand. She returned to her needlework with a thoughtful look on her face.

"Well, you must be starving. Go on upstairs and change out of that rumpled dress and I'll have the kitchen send something up. Join us when you're finished."

She waved me off and I obeyed her commands.

Half an hour and half a sandwich later I brought paper and a fresh pencil down to the veranda. "I thought I'd write a letter to my godmother and then look at my new library book," I explained.

At the word *godmother* Mrs. Harrington winced, her disapproval of Aunt Rachel totally transparent on her face. But she quickly wiped the reaction away.

"Of course, dear. What a splendid idea. We won't distract you. I'll have the waiter bring you some tea. Isn't this heat dreadful? . . ."

On my way past, Hannah's sharp eyes caught mine and made me pause. "Did you know the park's reopened?" she said. She gestured to her mother's maid, who stood silently behind her. "Charlotte told me so. I wanted us to go today but Mother says it's too late now."

"We'll go tomorrow, dear, tomorrow," Mrs. Harrington said, clearly undisturbed by having to put the event off another day. "I'm sure Garnet can manage to come home before the hottest part of the day tomorrow. Am I right, Garnet?"

"Yes, of course. I'd love to go."

"I heard a nasty rumor," Mrs. Harrington continued, and I stiffened at the words, "that they've got plans to sink the *Minnehaha* this month. Nobody cares about the beautiful old steamers anymore. I for one would like to take a last ride before they send it down."

I nodded in sympathy and relief and went to settle myself at the table.

I could feel Hannah's eyes boring into my back. Could she tell that I'd been lying about where I'd been? Had Charlotte seen something? What did Hannah know? I ignored her and pretended nothing was amiss as I picked up my pencil and thanked the waiter for the tea.

I looked out across the street to the grassy shoreline and the lake beyond and tried to gather my thoughts about the last two weeks. Finally, I could get them all out; I'd always been able to tell Aunt Rachel everything. I put the pencil to the page and easily filled it with neat script, telling her about the grand hotel, my new job, going to the amusement park on my own . . . I even told her about meeting Isabella, despite the fact that I didn't know exactly what to say. *I promised her I'd go see her at the dance hall even though I know I don't belong there and it would be so risky to go. Something about this girl makes me want to promise things. I'll wait a little while, at least. Hannah was suspicious today and I can't risk another lie just yet.*

I finished up the long letter and folded it four times before tucking it safely into the deep pocket of my dress. Then I took out the bird book from the library and flipped to the scarlet tanager, memorizing the solitary bird's migration patterns, plumage variations, nesting habits, diet, and life cycle. I did the same for the ring-billed gull afterward, laughing at how plain and ordinary it seemed in contrast to the beautiful tanager. Like me standing next to Isabella in the hat shop. I wondered when I'd be able to give her the image I'd cut out for her. How long would I have to wait before I'd be able to sneak out to the dance hall to see her?

My chance came much sooner than I'd expected.

I excused myself from the Harringtons' trip to the amusement park the next day with a genuine headache. While they picnicked at the pavilion and toured the lake in the *Minnehaha*, I lay in bed with the drapes tightly shut, accepting ice packs and little round pills from Charlotte every couple of hours. I joined them for dinner when they returned, feeling a little weak but mostly better, and listened to Hannah chatter about what a lovely time they'd had.

We all turned in early after such an "exhausting" day, and immediately I fell into a strangely vivid dream about Teddy.

We were in his car, alone, and he was kissing me and kissing me. "We should go to the movie," I said between kisses. "Alice and Adam are waiting for us."

"Not just yet," he said. "There's something I want to do first." Then he was on me and all over me and I knew with every inch of my skin that I didn't want this I didn't want this I didn't want this. I fought him, my hands flailing, my stomach twisting and crawling up into my throat. He caught my scream in his mouth and I lost the battle, going limp in his iron embrace, trying to think of something else.

But then the scene changed, like a light switch flipping in my head, and suddenly the arms around me were soft and white and the lips pulling back from mine were red—*red*.

Isabella laughed that chirping laugh and slipped out of the car and started to run. "Wait, wait for me," I called. I followed her but she was too quick. I lost her in a crowd of people pressing into a big building. "What is this place?" I asked some faceless person.

"The dance hall, of course."

I snapped awake. The dance hall. Of course. Now.

Silently, I pulled my nightgown off and a dress on, and I tiptoed out of the hotel suite with my shoes in one hand. Not a sound came from the Harringtons' bedrooms to change my mind.

"Out so late, Miss Garnet?" the bellboy said from behind the front desk as I rushed through the lobby.

"Can't sleep. Just going out for a walk."

"Of course, Miss."

Then, in blurred dreamtime moments, I was pressing into the Saturday night crowd at the dance hall and making my way toward the stage. People talked to me—men with deep voices, women with a tang on their breath—but I kept moving. Shimmying bodies danced like ghosts in the dim light, and jazz pulsed deliriously from the very floor of the place.

And there she was, on the stage, all sequins and fringe, bouncing out the most joyful Charleston I'd ever seen. Her costume shook and shuddered with the rhythm of it, and those bright lips matched that brand new slouched hat in a sassy red smile. The song ended I don't know how many minutes later, and as she took her bow her eyes met mine. She nodded me toward the side door that was open to the outside. The band took up a slow bluesy song and I followed Isabella's sparkling shape out the door.

Back in the fresh air again, I finally realized what I'd done. This was not a dream. I'd actually wandered out, at night, alone, into the drunken revelry of the dance hall. It was crazy. Bold. Dangerous. *Dangerous.* I shouldn't be here.

"Hey, sweetheart," Isabella said, lighting a cigarette. "Want a smoke?"

"No, no thank you."

"I'm glad you came out to see me. I wasn't so sure you'd make it. Avery said you were sick today."

"Avery?"

"The doorman over at the Galpin. He's a good friend of mine." Friends with a colored servant? Everything about this girl broke the rules. "He stopped in to say hi today and I asked if he knew you since you're staying there and all. He said you were laid up and your aunt was here at the park without you. I hope it wasn't serious."

She'd asked after me. She'd thought about me and asked after me and worried about me. My heart filled with that knowledge and I almost forgot to respond to her concern.

"It was just a headache. But I went to the park on my own yesterday. It was wonderful."

"Good." She blew out smoke and rested her elbow on her hip, the cigarette holder held out elegantly to the side like she'd been smoking all her life. Neither of us spoke for a minute and it was long enough for me to turn bashful, feeling ridiculous for coming out here. But then her hands were on my shoulders and she was turning me around and pointing up.

"Look at that moon," she said. It was full, pale, perfect.

"Makes me want to howl," I giggled, forgetting myself completely with her hands on me.

"So howl," she said. "Ouwwwooo!"

But I couldn't. I turned back to her, shaking my head.

"Here. Have some of this. Then howl." She reached down and pulled a tiny flask out of nowhere. It must have been tucked into her garter.

"What is it?"

"Gin."

"Um . . ." Was I really reaching for it? What was I thinking? Oh, my god, was I really going to— "Okay." I lifted the flask to my lips and sipped. The gin went down like fire. I sputtered. Then I turned and let out a feeble "Ooooww" toward that glorious moon. Even I knew it deserved better. Isabella laughed and nudged me. I took another tiny sip and tried again. *"Oooouuwww!"*

"That's better."

"I have something for you." I pulled the gull's silhouette out of my pocket and handed it to her. "From the park yesterday."

"You made this? For me?"

"For you."

"I don't know what to say. Thank you. The gulls are such a menace at the park, aren't they? Won't let you eat your popcorn in peace. But this is beautiful—perfect. How do you . . ."

My vision blurred and tipped a little. I blinked and it cleared.

"I have to go," I said, handing back the flask. "I shouldn't be here."

"Can I see you again?" she asked. "After work some day?"

"Sure. I'm done at noon."

"I'll meet you at the lake. Thursday. Down near the beach, at the three big rocks. Have you ever been fishing?"

"No."

"Well then, that settles it. And hey, if you're ever worried about sneaking in and out of the hotel, use the back entrance by the kitchens. They'll cover for you—just tell them you're Isabella's friend. Avery will watch out for you too."

She winked at me, tucked the flask and the cutout away beneath her dress, and stubbed out her cigarette. She turned to go back inside—the slow song was sighing to a close.

"Hey, Isabella," I called after her, curiosity getting the better of me. She looked back. "How old are you?"

"Eighteen in September," she said. "But don't tell them that." She gestured to the white-shirted men who stood near the stage, overseeing the show and the crowd like huge pelicans collectively foraging for a meal. One of them glanced over at Isabella and I could swear he looked hungry. And all at once I knew what that pang under my ribs was. Hunger. Isabella seemed to have that effect on people, and I was not spared.

"Really, Garnet," she said, reaching back and wrapping her hand around my wrist. "Don't tell anyone. If they knew I was underage they'd kick me off that stage in a heartbeat."

Then she was gone. Before I could even promise I'd never tell. But my wrist still burned where she'd touched me.

One of the pelican men was moving toward the side door. If Isabella was too young to be here, I was *far* too young. I couldn't let him see me. I ran.

I didn't stop running until I reached the door of the hotel suite. Then I silently tiptoed to my room, undressed, and with my heart pounding, dropped into bed.

Howling at the moon and drinking gin with Isabella and getting away with two secret excursions in two days must have given me some kind of crazy courage, because on Monday when I went back to work, I got up the nerve to say something to Miss Maple about the feathers.

I crouched in the window, arranging a display of straw sunhats as she handed them to me. I pointed out a pheasant feather on one hat, a feather I knew hadn't been shed naturally like the ones I used to find with Daddy.

"They kill hundreds—thousands—of birds for these feathers," I told her. "It's illegal, but they do it anyway. It's good money. Some of these species are going extinct. A lot of women refuse to wear real feathers in their hats now, you know."

"A lot of women won't buy a hat without them, though, and I have a business to run," she said, handing me a flounce-brimmed one with a lacy ribbon. "Besides, there are always more birds. We couldn't possibly kill them all."

I knew that was faulty logic. The extinction of the messenger pigeon had proven that we could, in fact, wipe out an entire species through unregulated hunting. Any Junior Audubon Society member knew that, and I'd been a member since Father signed me up when I was six and we did the Christmas Count together. I still cherished the pair of mailorder binoculars that came with the membership.

But how could I explain all that to Miss Maple? Especially without losing my job?

"By the way, how was your Fourth of July, dear?" Miss Maple asked, changing the subject. "Did you catch the fireworks last night?"

"We watched from the hotel veranda. Quite a show. I'd never seen so many at once. Like big bouquets of flowers in the sky . . . But about the feathers, Miss Maple—"

A customer came in then, and my efforts were cut short. It was a start, though, and I felt good about bringing it up. At least now she knew it was an issue, even if she wouldn't admit it was a problem. Progress. I'd just have to sell customers non-feathered hats as best I could in the meantime.

I hopped down from the finished display and admired it with my hands on my hips. The multilevel arrangement of wheat-gold hats had a pleasing, midsummer-abundance feel to it. I was getting good at building displays. I was also getting good at helping customers.

"Why don't you go get lunch, Miss Maple. I'll help Mrs. Anderson."

"Thank you, dear. I think I will. She's looking for a

church hat to go with her new lavender suit." And she was looking at feathered ones.

"These are lovely, Mrs. Anderson," I said, leading her toward another stand. "Silk flowers in the bands are very popular you know, and look! Lilacs! How perfect. Let's see if this fits you. No? Too tight? I think I've got another in back. Just one minute . . ."

The days that followed stretched out lazily as I waited for my Thursday date with Isabella. I worked in the mornings, spent my afternoons on the veranda with the Harringtons or walking by the lake, and devoted evenings to studying every natural history and environmental science book the Excelsior Library could dig up for me. Having the time and freedom to sift through them was such a luxury; the lingering twilight soon became my favorite time of day.

I also wrote letters and received letters during those long days, and if I hadn't been so content with my work and leisure time and so looking forward to Thursday, the news from home would have been truly distressing.

Mother assured me that Father was really making a lot of progress and all would be well before I got home, despite, she said, "some trouble at work." What did that mean? Should I let myself hope for his recovery? Aunt Rachel said that Sarah was having health problems and most of her time was spent nursing these days. Alice wrote to invite me to, of all things, her *wedding*, which was set for October! She and Adam just couldn't wait any longer, she said, so she'd decided not to go back to school in the fall. No need, she explained, since her future was now secure and she just couldn't wait to start having babies. Even Teddy wrote a simple but kind letter to say he missed me and he was excited to go to the pictures with me once I got back to the city in August. He had an important question to ask me, he said, and he underlined *important*, as if I really needed another hint about what he meant to ask and how he expected me to answer. Then he signed the letter "Your Teddy."

. Finally, Mother passed along my grades. I smiled to see the As in literature, French, history, and biology, and I cringed a little at the B- in typing and shorthand. I'd taken that class only because Alice thought she might get a summer job in an office and she wanted company. But it was dull work, and two weeks into it I wished I'd carried on with mathematics. *This coming year,* I thought, *calculus.* Then I remembered that Alice wouldn't be at school, and wouldn't even try to talk me into taking chorus or sewing or Raising a Model Citizen. I laughed a little and wiped away a tear.

Then I saw the note from my biology teacher underneath the grades. "I'd be happy to give you a recommendation to go to the university next year," it read in his compact script. "Please stop by once school starts up again to chat with me about your plans for after graduation."

My heart skipped. Then it sobered instantly when I saw the cheery comment Mother had clipped next to his words: "We know what your plans will be!" She may as well have drawn wedding bells underneath.

In seven weeks I'd be heading home to confront all those things—family, friends, school, my future—but August twenty-sixth still felt like a long way off. I shook the thoughts away and instead focused on looking forward to Thursday.

Great Egret
(*Ardea alba*)

Finally, Thursday arrived. I'd warned Mrs. Harrington that I'd be spending the entire afternoon at the library and she should not expect me for lunch, so after work I headed directly for the lakeshore. The three rocks where I was to meet Isabella for an afternoon of fishing stood near the beaches, a ways up the shoreline from the Galpin House. I was pretty sure I'd be out of sight from the hotel's veranda once I got there, but the walk took me right past it, and I prayed the Harringtons were safely at their lunch in the dining room as I hurried by.

The bellboy was helping a petite elderly woman up the front steps. He looked up and caught my eye. *Oh, no! He saw me!* Panic stopped me in my tracks.

Then he winked.

I stared at him, flustered. A colored man *winked* at me? What was I supposed to do?

After a moment of gaping and blinking stupidly, I did the only thing I could do: I smiled and nodded and scurried past.

It had all taken no more than a few seconds, but I mulled it over for the rest of the walk. Finally, I resolved to ignore the unsettled feeling in my stomach. The bellboy—no, she'd called him a *doorman* and the term was clearly much more dignified—the doorman was a friend of Isabella's and that made him a friend of mine. Besides, he was the cormorant who'd helped us all through the hailstorm and I'd liked him from the beginning; I'd just never thought of him as someone to make friends with. But I needed all the friends I could get if I was going to keep seeing Isabella in secret—and I had every intention of doing just that.

Okay then, I thought. *The doorman. Avery.*

I hardly recognized Isabella dressed in pants and without lipstick.

The pants were rolled up almost to the knee, showing off firm, bare calves and little-girl feet, and she wore a sleeveless blouse with two buttons open at the neck. She managed to look grown-up in whatever she wore, even though she was hardly older than me.

How does she stay so pale? I wondered, staring at the milky white collarbones that she thought nothing of exposing to the harsh summer sun. *It must be in her blood.*

I felt silly in my dress and sun hat as I joined her on the rocks and I told her so.

"Nonsense, you look beautiful," she said. Then she set

me up with a pole. I tried to imitate her casual posture, tried to hold the fishing pole in that comfortable, careless way that she was holding hers. It was just like the cigarette holder the other night—the thing just *belonged* with her; it was a part of her body that she carried with ease and confidence. I wondered if I looked like that with a sewing needle or a soup ladle, and I shuddered a little at the thought.

"I'm glad you got away," she said after a minute, looking out over the water. "Does your aunt know where you are?"

"Oh, no. She thinks I'm at the library."

Isabella laughed, "And does she approve of *that?*"

"I'm starting to think she doesn't approve of anything. Except herself of course. And her daughter."

"Well, naturally. I know her type. They're the ones that send the police to the dance hall every other night claiming that we're 'disturbing the peace.' The managers hate that and so do I. You'll have peace when you're dead, that's what I say. I bet she doesn't care for books because 'they give young girls all kinds of crazy ideas.' How many times have I heard that one? But I suppose books are more wholesome and refined companions for you than I am, right?"

"That's the general idea . . ." I squirmed in my seat on the rock. "But please don't think, you know *I* don't, I mean—"

"Of course not, Garnet, don't worry. I'm flattered, actually, to be considered a bad influence. You don't think I got my reputation by chance, do you?"

I laughed.

"Do you think other hotel guests will see me out here

and tell Mrs. Harrington?" I said, looking up and down the shoreline.

"Someone might see you. And some of them are gossips, I'm sure. But most of them will be too caught up in their own outings on a warm, sunny day like this to be worried about you. You'd be amazed how self-involved people can be."

I sighed, shrugged. I was determined to enjoy this time with Isabella, despite the risk.

"Plus, from what I hear, plenty of people don't much care for your aunt. So it's not as though the town is crawling with her spies. But let's be quiet now," she said. "We're frightening the fish."

We sat there silently with our lines in the water for a long time and I could feel her beside me even though we didn't touch. The fish weren't biting but I didn't mind—I could've waited all afternoon like that.

But then a great egret swooped low and landed in the shallows not fifteen feet down the shore from us. Bright white, slender, and elegant, it stalked its prey from above on stiltlike legs. Now and then it plunged its sharp beak into the water and surfaced with a small, struggling fish or frog clamped in its bill. It swallowed the creatures whole. The egret was so beautiful and so fierce that I couldn't help myself—I slowly set down my fishing pole and reached into my pocket for scissors and paper. I began to cut. Gradually, the bird's dark twin emerged from the paper.

Isabella looked dismayed that I'd given up on my pole to watch our highly skilled neighbor fish instead. But, intrigued, she turned to watch me as the image took shape in my hands. I felt her eyes on me.

"How *do* you do that?" she asked, her line still in the water. When I'd snipped back the last of the tail feathers, I pulled out a clean sheet and handed it to her, along with my scissors.

"Do you want to try? Be careful with these; the points are sharper than they look."

Reluctantly, she reeled in her line and set her pole down next to mine. She took the crane scissors from me and turned them over and over in her hand. She touched them with reverence, as though she'd never held anything so delicate in her life, running her slender fingers over the handles, the crane's arched body, the hinge, the blades.

I shivered despite the heat.

"My mother gave them to me so I wouldn't dull my sewing scissors on paper. I was twelve. Father had just come home from the war and it was clear he wouldn't be taking my side and helping me get back to real birding. So I make these."

"They're divine. And your mother, she encourages this I hope?"

"Yes. She prefers it to the alternative—collecting specimens and things like that. But here's what she doesn't know." I took out the chalk and labeled the bird *Ardea alba*.

"Latin names. I saw that on the gull you gave me. You're a scientist as well as an artist then, I see." I blushed. "Okay. You tried fishing, so I'll give this a try." She took the paper from me and looked down into the water. A small

77

sunny drifted just below the surface. Tiny minnows darted anxiously around it, but it seemed to sense that we'd given up fishing for the moment, and it treaded water calmly. It practically posed for Isabella.

A minute later, she'd hacked a fish shape out of the black paper—an oval with tail fins and pouting lips. "It's no use," she said. "I'm terrible at this." She crumpled the paper in her hand and tried to give the scissors back. I didn't take them. Instead, I pulled another fresh sheet out of my over-sized pocket.

I'd never tried to put it into words before. I looked to the great white bird for help as I set out to explain a new way of seeing.

"You can't just look at it and say 'it's an egret' and then try to cut the shape of an egret," I told her, thinking it out as I went. "You have to see it differently. You have to follow its edges and know that it's only an egret because it *isn't* water or sky or beach. It's an egret because it has boundaries."

I looked back to her and she knit her perfectly shaped eyebrows together. "Boundaries? I don't think I follow you."

I took a deep breath, turning my eyes back to the bird. "You have to look for the borders between things and trace those dividing lines without thinking that you know what an egret is, or what a cormorant is, or what a grouse is. It'll surprise you every time when the silhouette turns out looking real—like you just snatched the bird's shadow from under its feet."

"But don't the birds move?"

I smiled. "That's what makes it a challenge. You just have to be quiet and not startle them, like a real field biologist." I pointed to the egret and said, "Look—she posed for me, and she stayed here fishing with us this long." Isabella still seemed interested, so I went on. "Scientists used to kill birds in order to study them, you know. They shot them down and stuffed them, and then they made their drawings and took their measurements. Modern scientists have been trying to study birds from life, like we are. It was Audubon who changed all that."

"Audubon?"

"He was an ornithologist. He pointed out that scientists were doing more damage than good with the way they were studying birds. Showed them another way. I've been a Junior Audubon Society member since I was six. Father and I used to do all kinds of excursions. Then Aunt Rachel would take me while he was away at war even though Mother didn't like it. I thought Father would start up again when he came home—but it didn't happen that way."

"Why don't you go with Rachel anymore?"

What was I doing? Why was I telling her all this? "Mother thinks it's time for me to be a lady . . . and Father doesn't really trust his sister, I don't think. But at least he speaks to her. The rest of his family cut her off when she moved in with Sarah. I'll bet Mrs. Harrington wouldn't even admit to being related to Aunt Rachel—her own first cousin."

"'Moved in with Sarah,' you said? Is that her lover?" Isabella's voice was casual. The word *lover* took me by surprise and then sank in slowly.

"I suppose so. We never really talk about it that way. I guess my parents still like to consider it a Victorian friendship. They saw it differently in their time. Intimacy between women was just, well, normal. Now everyone thinks it's a scandal. Sarah is just Aunt Rachel's family, and we all know that. But I suppose they are . . . lovers."

We were quiet for a moment, watching the waves. I turned the word over and over in my mind: *lovers . . . lovers . . . lovers . . .* My skin tingled.

"Anyway," I said, shaking the word out of my head and handing Isabella the sheet of paper I still held, "pretend you've never seen a sunfish before, and look again. This kind of thing takes practice, so I'll practice fishing while you try a second time." I grabbed my pole and moved a little ways away so I wouldn't frighten Isabella's subject. And so my hands would stop trembling. I moved a little too quickly, though, and the egret shot me a suspicious glance. Then she flapped her wings and glided down the shore another twenty feet.

I cast my line back into the water. The rocks made a rough seat and the sun glared down at me. I'd left my hat back with Isabella. But I barely noticed any discomfort as I gazed out at the lake and watched the sailboats drift like white clouds across the blue. I thought about egrets and fathers and aunts and beautiful girls in pants, and I thought about how many kinds of love there are in the world.

The egret caught four or five courses of lunch in her new fishing spot. Isabella caught a decently rendered image of the sunny, and then put her line back in and caught the sunny himself, in celebration. "You're not even a snack," she said before releasing him again. I caught nothing, except maybe another freckle or two from the bright sun.

"Do you want an ice cream?" Isabella asked, coming to join me on my rock. Midday had turned to afternoon and sweat had begun to collect at my temples. My stomach growled in protest over missing lunch. There was nothing I wanted more than an ice cream.

But would Hannah be suspicious if I was gone too long? Would she tell her mother? If Mrs. Harrington knew I was out fishing with the dance hall girl she'd surely write to Mother. And what would Mother do? Tell Mrs. Harrington to keep a closer watch on me? Tell me to quit my job because it was clearly giving me improper ideas? Tell me to come home this instant so that she could keep me on a short leash for the rest of the summer, or the rest of my life? I could not let those things happen. I had to be careful.

Then Isabella reached up with her soft fingers and tucked a flyaway tendril behind my ear. My heart hiccuped in my chest.

"I'm buying," I said, reeling in my line.

Chipping Sparrow
(*Spizella passerina*)

"Tell me about your family, Isabella," I said once we were settled under the picnic pavilion with our ice creams. Isabella had taken me there the long way, through the streets behind the hotel, so we wouldn't have to pass in front of it on our way to the park. We hadn't seen any other hotel guests yet, but I didn't want to push my luck. My eyes skimmed right and left around the pavilion—no one I recognized. I was safe for the moment and determined to enjoy my ice cream.

I'd chosen strawberry. She'd picked chocolate mint.

"Do you have brothers and sisters?" I asked.

"Brothers," she said. "Plenty of them." Then she stopped herself.

"Just tell me what you want to," I said. "I don't mean to pry. I just . . . I want to know you."

"I'll tell you anything. Everything, if you want to hear

it. I just wasn't sure how to start. Let's see." She paused a moment, gathered her thoughts, and continued. "I ran away from home when I turned fifteen," she said. *She ran away!* I stared at her, wide eyed, and gestured for her to continue. "My parents live up on the Iron Range; my dad works in the mines. My mom is Lutheran, very Lutheran. She's also very controlling. And very unhappy. I have four brothers, all younger than me. David, John, Andrew, and Michael—well, Mitch."

I wanted to ask about running away. What was it like? How did she do it? Was she scared? But instead, I let her continue the thread she'd started. "What are they like, your brothers?" I asked.

"Well, the older ones are all pretty much the same: tough, bossy, stupid. They're just going to end up in the mines and they don't even care. But little Mitch—he's different.".

Her face changed then. The carefree air about her had settled into a deep thoughtfulness. She loved this brother, that was easy enough to tell, but there was something else there too.

"He wants to be a boxer, like Jack Dempsey. I'm sure it's partly because he wants to be stronger and tougher than he is with all those big brothers always pushing him around. But I think it's mostly because he wants to go out into the world and do big things." She smiled to herself, remembering him. "He loves the radio, and maps, and he wants his mother to be proud of him. He wants—wanted—*me* to be proud of him."

Then I *had* to ask: "Do you regret it?"

"What?"

"Running away."

"No! Heavens, no. I love the freedom. And I'm doing pretty well for myself with the dancing. At least, *this* is a really good gig. There were other places that, well, that weren't so nice as this." Her body stiffened, then with a deep breath she relaxed again. "Now things are better. I'm happy I left. But Mitch—I regret leaving him behind. I just don't know if he'll ever make it out of there like I did."

She went to work on her ice cream then; it had been melting while she talked. "I'm babbling," she said through a bite of chocolate mint. "Tell me about you."

"Nothing to tell, really. Nothing exciting."

"I don't believe that for a minute. What are you doing out here for the summer, for instance? With this crazy aunt of yours, or whoever she is?"

So I told her everything. About Mother and Father and the war; about Alice and Adam; about Teddy and the hope chest; and finally about Mrs. Harrington and Hannah and the hat shop. When I stopped to finish off the tip of my ice cream cone Isabella said, "What about the birds? I mean, you're passionate about them, right?"

"Well, yes. In some other life, I'd maybe go to college and study science. Keep the Miss Maples of the world from allowing beautiful creatures to be killed off in the name of fashion." I laughed.

"Some other life, huh?" She wasn't laughing.

"Oh, my mother would never let me. I'm supposed to get married and have babies and run a steady middle-class household like a good girl." I told her about the note from my biology teacher, and she stared at me in disbelief.

"Why don't you run away?" she said. She was serious.

I licked strawberry from my fingers and thought about it.

"I suppose because I love them, you know? My family. I want to do right by them. I want them to think well of me. I want to make decisions that will make them happy too."

And there I felt the conversation, and possibly our friendship, grind to a halt.

Her face turned blank and stony; her eyes hardened.

"I don't mean . . . Oh, Isabella, I'm sorry. I'm not criticizing you. I'm sure you made the right decision for you. I admire you for doing what you love—I really do. You're a beautiful dancer." She just looked at me and looked at me. I withered.

A long moment passed as a little girl chased her brother in circles around the picnic tables. The roller coaster clattered by overhead. A streetcar boat sounded its deafening whistle down at the docks. Isabella just looked at me with those hard, dark eyes.

Finally, I got up from the table. "I'll go," I said. I got four whole miserable steps away before she called out to me in a small, sad voice I could hardly tell was hers.

"Do you really think . . ." I turned, with a heavy sigh of relief still mixed with worry. But the stone face had crumbled around the edges and the eyes were glossy with tears behind them. "Do you really think that I'm a—a—beautiful dancer?"

"Of course," I said. "You're like. . . fireworks."

And the tension broke into a hundred pieces at our feet.

"Can I see you again?" she said, dabbing at the corners of her eyes with the napkin from her ice cream cone.

"Anytime you want. Just come by the shop, or have Avery give me a note."

"I will. Soon."

"Okay." Then I turned to go because I was grinning so hard I thought my face would crack. I knew I probably looked like a fool and I had to get out of there before I embarrassed myself further.

"And Garnet?" she said. I composed my face as well as I could and turned back. "What is that?" She pointed to a little brown bird that hopped around under the picnic table, feasting on crumbs.

"Just a chipping sparrow," I said without hesitation. "Why?"

She smiled. "Just wondering." She laughed that chattering laugh as I headed off toward the hotel with a sparrow's quick steps and a light heart.

Halfway back to the hotel I saw Mrs. Granger from room 304 with her small son. I smiled and waved hello, relieved that the sighting I'd been nervous about all day had happened *after* I'd said good-bye to Isabella. My luck had held.

Isabella was true to her word. The very next afternoon as I sat with the Harringtons on the veranda, Avery brought me a note on a little silver tray.

I'm out back. I want to take you flying. We'll only be gone an hour. Please come?

Flying?

"The librarian has a new book for me," I told Mrs. Harrington. "I'm going to go pick it up. I'll only be out for a bit."

"Fine, fine," she mumbled, and she returned to the crossword puzzle in the daily paper. She'd been at the thing for an hour and seemed to be making little progress.

"Would you pick up some yellow thread for me in town?" Hannah asked. "I've run out."

"Of course." I flashed her an innocent smile, and within two minutes I was out the front door and headed around to the back of the hotel to meet Isabella.

She took me on the carousel. Exactly one week earlier, when I'd snuck off to the park on my own, I'd looked longingly at the carousel but decided against it. I felt too silly to ride it alone. Climbing aboard with Isabella the following Friday felt perfect.

It was a drab, cloudy day, but the painted horses shone under the ride's thousand lights as we climbed on. I tried to sit in a carriage seat, but she insisted I ride the over-and-under horse next to hers—a white horse with a red bridle and a swept-back mane that made it look to be in motion even when it stood still. I rode sidesaddle, both appalled by and jealous of my pants-wearing companion, who rode her horse like a man. The ticket taker started at the single red lightbulb fixed into the ceiling among all the clear bulbs and worked his way around to us. My change purse was on the bureau in my room at the hotel. "No free rides," he said in a gruff voice.

Thankfully, Isabella had the fare for us both. "I'm taking

you flying, remember?" she said. Then the Sousa march started up and the horses came alive.

We flew.

"My thread?" Hannah asked when I returned to the veranda.

I'd forgotten. I remembered to pick up a library book only because Isabella asked on our way to the hotel what excuse I'd come up with. But I'd completely forgotten about Hannah's yellow thread.

She saw me falter.

She glanced around. We were alone—her mother had gone into the lobby to listen to the radio. "I don't know what you're up to, but you're up to something," she said quietly with her thin lips in a sneer.

"Nonsense. I just left my purse," I said, shocked that it was the truth that saved me. "I'll go get it now and fetch you some thread, Hannah. I'm sorry."

I dodged her pointed glare and scurried off to grab my purse and run the errand, my mind buzzing the whole way into town. Hannah was suspicious. Mrs. Harrington, I could tell, had given me up for a lost cause and didn't care what I did as long as I went to work in the mornings, stayed out of trouble in the afternoons, found my way back to the hotel by dinner, and went to bed at a "Christian" hour. In fact, she seemed to like that I was out of her hair most of the time and away from her impressionable daughter, who I could do nothing to improve and who could not, therefore, benefit from my company in the least. She would never have approved of what I was doing, so I simply didn't tell her. She lived under the happy assumption that I spent my afternoons walking at the lake or holed up at the library, and she didn't bother herself about it much. Hannah was not so easily fooled. Though until she knew what to tell on me *for*, I didn't think she would say anything to her mother.

But if I snuck out every day and constantly risked being seen by other hotel guests and confused my own mind with constant lying, Hannah would be sure to find out what I was doing and whom I was doing it with. So I would need to be more careful. I would need to wait awhile before seeing Isabella again.

The thought set off a pang inside me—Isabella was joy and excitement and adventure and everything else seemed dull in comparison—but there was no way around it.

After I delivered the thread I excused myself to my room. I wrote a note telling Isabella that I was sorry but I needed a little time to let Hannah's suspicion subside before we went out together again. I rang for Avery, our willing messenger, and asked him to deliver it.

He noticed my long face when he took the note from me at the door of the suite.

"Does the girl know?" he asked, his voice hesitant to address me so informally.

But formality at this point seemed ridiculous. He was a friend now, at least when the Harringtons weren't watching.

"Not yet. I want to keep it that way."

"Right, right. Well, let me know when you think it's safe. I'll fetch her for you."

I smiled.

"She's a gem, isn't she," he said. "Our Bella?"

"The best."

He turned to go.

"Avery?" I said. He turned in the hallway. "Thank you."

"No problem, Miss."

I swallowed hard and then corrected him. "Garnet."

He paused, then looked right and left. The hall was empty. His eyes came up to meet mine and he nodded once. Then he said, in a low voice, "Right, Garnet."

I closed the door slowly and then leaned back on it. After a moment of pouting I went back to my room and set myself up at the writing desk, vowing to stay occupied for a few days or maybe even a week. I'd catch up on my reading, I decided, and my correspondence. There was so much trouble going on at home and I'd hardly thought to worry myself with any of it since meeting Isabella. Now it rushed back to me and I felt compelled to send reassuring and distracting letters to my parents, to Aunt Rachel, to Alice, to Teddy. I started with my parents, composing for them a happy letter about the lake and the weather and my harmless little job and the progress of my needlepoint. It seemed like fiction. Like writing about another life. Another girl.

I'd just have to pretend to be that other girl for a while, until Hannah stopped looking at me with questions in her eyes every time I set foot outside the hotel. And even though that other girl was the girl I'd been for years, being her now was like acting a part in a play.

Actually, I thought, *it was always like acting a part in a play. I just didn't realize it.*

Red-Tailed Hawk
(*Buteo jamaicensis*)

During that long week of self-imposed estrangement from Isabella, the hat shop was my refuge. Oddly, the fussy little store with its mother-hen proprietor and its constant stream of feminine customers liberated me from what I'd always thought of as the woman's world. There, I was free from the confinement of "home," free from idle hours and dull company and mundane work. My hands were kept busy unpacking boxes and arranging displays and handling money; my mind was always occupied helping customers and making change and tallying receipts; my quiet nature was stretched by the constant interactions with strangers and as I learned to navigate the unique relationship between employee and boss.

The job served as a distraction from so many things— the troubles I heard about in letters from home (and the progress that I didn't dare believe in), the difficulties of living with the Harringtons, the knowledge that my time with Isabella was limited and already slipping away, and the decisions (especially the answer to an *important* question) I would have to make once I arrived home at the end of the summer, a mere six weeks away. But the job was much more than a distraction, too. The work filled me up with a sense of competence, gave me a taste of precious independence. I loved it.

Finally, as Friday rolled around again and a full week had passed since I'd seen Isabella, I darted out of work at noon and rushed down to the docks. The lake sparkled in the full summer sunlight, wavelets dancing, inviting me on the day's long-awaited adventure. And there was Isabella, sitting on the second dock just like we'd planned through a series of secret notes, dangling her bare feet in the water. She smiled up at me as I approached and it was marvelously clear—she'd missed me as much as I'd missed her.

Maybe she had longed for a companion as much as I had—come to think of it, she'd never mentioned other friends besides Avery. Was it possible that this beautiful, talented, outgoing girl was actually lonely? Or, could it be true that she felt the same tug beneath her ribs when I was near her that I felt when she was near me? Her longings were a mystery to me. I could hardly get a handle on my own.

"You know, I've never stolen anything before," I said as I joined her on the dock, still nervous about what we'd planned to do. "Is this it?" I eyed the little dinghy tied beside her. It didn't seem like much. She'd assured me that the owner had a new speedboat and didn't care a bit for this old piece of tin. He'd never notice it was gone, she had promised me that.

"Yeah, this is it. Isn't she perfect?" Isabella said, her eyes shining, reflecting the gleaming water.

"I guess," I said.

"Get in." She tossed her satchel, our picnic, into the bottom of the boat and climbed in after it.

I hesitated.

She laughed and held a hand out to me. I tentatively reached one foot out over the edge of the dock as I grasped her soft hand. I closed my eyes and leapt into the boat. It rocked beneath me and in a quick move Isabella guided me onto a bench. She'd obviously done this before. I wished then that I'd been raised in the country, but I didn't for a moment voice my jealousy to the girl who'd grown up with too many siblings in a too-small house with too little money. I watched her unwind the rope from the dock with ease and toss it into the bottom of the boat. Then she sat down herself and grabbed the oars.

"How can you possibly have such soft hands?" I asked. She looked so feminine and yet she could fish and row and carry on like a man.

"I have to grease them up at night and sleep with gloves on. Disgusting, isn't it?"

"The best of both worlds," I countered, as she bent to work.

I'd been in boats before. A girl can't grow up in

Minnesota without spending at least some time on the water. But I'd never been in one like this—a rusty tin can of a boat, so low on the water that there was nothing but a sheet of metal between my feet and the lake.

As we pushed off from the dock the dinghy swayed gently on the waves and then surged forward as Isabella pulled on the oars. She was stronger than she looked. I held onto the ridges on either side of the boat with white-knuckled hands at first, but my grip relaxed as I got used to the rhythmic rock and surge of the little craft.

Isabella smiled at me as she pulled the oars against the weight of the water. "Turn around," she said. Then she must have seen my grip tighten again because she added, "Just swing one leg over the seat at a time. Keep your weight low and we'll be fine. This old girl is sturdier than she seems."

I moved slowly, crouching down low in the boat. I swung one leg over the bench and then the other, my white skirt rubbing against the dusty metal. *What was I thinking wearing white today?* I thought, irritated with having decided to dress to allay Hannah's suspicions instead of dressing practically to suit the activity of the day. I'd stayed away from the library all week so that I could plausibly pretend to be spending the day there during this trip with Isabella. I couldn't think of any other excuse, so I'd hoped the old one would still work if I dressed the part. Hannah just shrugged when I told her and went back to her knitting; my plan to calm her suspicions by waiting awhile to sneak out again seemed to have worked. And thank heavens for that. If she were to guess, if she were to tell, I'd never have another adventure again. I'd be packed up and sent home, and this little flame of excitement that was suddenly lighting up my whole life would be snuffed out faster than a turn of the Ferris wheel.

Shaking the worry off, I settled myself in the exact center of the bench, facing front. Then I brought my eyes up from the rocking boat and looked out over the glittering water. I caught my breath at the glorious sight. My hat blew off my head and its ribbon caught it around my neck. My hair danced in the wind, leaping from my head and twirling in the air. The breeze was much stronger here, away from the shore.

There was nothing between me and this perfect panorama. I had always had flying dreams, and the carousel had come close to realizing them, but this—this was amazing. I squinted against the brightness of the reflected sun that bounced and played on the waves. And that smell, like the whole world was alive beneath the surface of this water, and calling to me to come back to the depths. I reached over the side and trailed my fingers in the cool water. Then I touched my wet fingertips to my forehead, where the skin was warm from the sun.

A red-tailed hawk circled high in the air, soaring effortlessly. I watched it, and for once I felt like I understood the easy dip and glide of hollow bones in flight. A memory surged back on me of being a little girl jumping off the kitchen step stool and flapping my arms against the air, trying to teach myself to fly. Sometimes I could swear I hovered a moment in midair, but I'd always ended up crashing to the ground. Daddy would laugh at me, his warm rumbling laugh, and say *Fly, Gigi, fly!* Then when I fell, he would dust off my knees and help me back up onto the stool. I was way too old for that kind of game now, but I never stopped wishing that someday I might feel that kind of lightness.

I pulled out paper and did my best to snip the hawk's gliding silhouette despite the motion of the boat. It was imperfect, but it would be enough to remind me of this day, when Isabella took me flying for the *second* time, without even meaning to.

We didn't speak during the row to Big Island. We were too busy feeling the sun on our skin and listening to the waves lap against the boat and watching the green blotch of land come nearer and nearer.

"Here we are," she said as we pulled alongside the island's shore. She leapt over the side of the boat and splashed into the shallows, dragging the dinghy up toward the land. "You might want to take off your shoes."

I unlaced my shoes and pulled off my stockings, lining them up under the bench seat and laying my hat on top. The air felt cool against my bare feet and calves. I bunched my skirt up in one fist and reached the other hand out to Isabella. The water chilled my feet and felt slippery against my ankles; my toes wriggled into the rough sand. Minnows skittered away from the intrusion.

Isabella squeezed my hand and then let it go so she could drag the little boat all the way up onto the sandy beach. Then she turned back to me where I stood in six inches of water, trying to be still enough to coax the minnows back.

"Come on," she said, laughing at the image of me courting the tiny fish. "There's something I want to show you."

Downy Woodpecker
(*Picoides pubescens*)

"You certainly know your way around," I told Isabella as we set off past the strip of sand, through a little clearing, and into the woods. "How long have you lived in Excelsior?"

"This is my second summer here. They were hiring performers last spring when the park first opened—I jumped at the chance to get out of St. Paul. Avery showed me around some, and I tromped around with the other new park workers. Mostly I've just explored a lot on my own. Last winter stretched on forever—the off-season is so dead out here that I had to wait tables in a tearoom for a while to get by—and when spring came this year I was desperate to get outside. I've been all over! I came out to Big Island earlier this week and found something I knew you had to see."

As we picked our way through the woods, every rock and twig jabbed into my too-soft feet, but I bit my lip and vowed not to complain and *not* to ask what kind of snakes lived in these woods. My dress caught on bushes and mosquitoes bit at my ankles, and part of me minded. It was habit, being concerned about those things. But another part of me, a deeper part, rejoiced in the dirt between my toes and the leaves in my hair. Before I could stop myself, I wished Daddy were here with me—the old Daddy who had always wished for a son but made do with a little girl instead.

"Where are we going?" I asked, stopping that train of thought before it could leave the station.

"Just follow me. It's a surprise."

We picked our way through the brush and at last came out in a large overgrown clearing littered with heaps of rusting metal and rotting wood. The place had a mournful feel about it, like a graveyard.

"What is this place?"

"The ruins of the old amusement park, the Big Island park that ran back when the huge steamboats ferried tourists around the lake. Not much left now." She looked out over the piles of scrap lumber and bent nails.

"Is this the surprise?"

"No, no," she said. "Almost there. Watch where you step."

At the edge of the rubbish piles she turned, stopped me, and put a hand over my eyes.

"Do you hear that?" she said. A dull *pik-pik* sound came from someplace overhead.

"A woodpecker?"

She moved her hand and pointed to a nearby elm tree. "Two," she said, pointing first at the little black-and-white flecked body that clung to the bark of the tree, and then at the nearly identical bird poking its head out of a hole farther up. The male's short bill rapped against the wood in search of bugs while his mate gazed down at him. "What kind are they?" Isabella asked.

"Downy woodpeckers. See the white patch on the back, and the red spot on the male's nape? They're too small to be hairy woodpeckers."

"Wow," Isabella said. "I've seen that kind before and I never knew what to call them."

She looked over at me, impressed, and I gave her a little shrug and a smile. I couldn't fish or row or dance, but it was nice to be the expert sometimes.

"They're a mated couple," I went on. "I'll bet they hatched four or five eggs in that hole earlier in the season. The little ones have probably flown off already, but the pair is still together."

"Do you like it?" she asked. "Your surprise?"

"They're beautiful."

But as I watched the pair of birds go about their domestic routine, little holes opened up in my chest, like the woodpeckers were drumming their beaks into my heart. What was happening? I'd been so looking forward to this day trip, so ready to enjoy some time with Isabella. So why did I feel like I was breaking into pieces just as we reached our destination?

"Aren't you going to cut out a silhouette?"

"No," I said, my voice choked. For once, I didn't feel like it. After a moment my heart was so full of holes I had to turn away. I took a few shaky steps away from the birds, away from the elm, away from Isabella. Then I stopped, steadying myself on a piece of roller coaster track, dizzy as I'd been after stepping out of the twisting tunnel on my first visit to the amusement park. I gazed out over the rubble of this old park and fought the tears down. It looked as though the whole world was in ruins. Somehow it had all fallen down around me while I was busy pretending and forgetting—lying and stealing and sneaking around.

My mind spun.

What was I doing here hiding in the woods with this smoking-drinking-dancing girl, watching a pair of happily mated birds while my family fell apart at home and my hope chest waited, half full and neglected. Maybe Isabella could run away from the people she cared about in order to live an unpredictable life without the solid safety of home—but I couldn't. I couldn't.

I shuddered with that thought, and tears overwhelmed me.

Then the idea struck me—I needed to write to Teddy, have him come for a visit, urge him to go ahead and ask me that important question. I couldn't wait six more weeks. It was the sixeenth of July and I'd gotten in enough trouble in the month since I'd arrived in Excelsior. Teddy needed to come. He needed to settle it, before I got carried away wishing for things that could never happen. I would write him as soon as I got back to the hotel. I had to.

I had to.

"What's wrong?" Isabella asked, approaching me slowly from the edge of the woods as though I was a wild animal she didn't want to frighten away. "Should I take you back?"

"Yes." Teddy. The hotel. Teddy. Yes. But then I faltered, my resolve vanishing as quickly as it had come. "No . . . I don't know."

The tears came faster.

Isabella laid a hand on my shoulder, and without another thought I threw myself into her arms. She held me a minute in silence and then pulled back to look at me, concern etched into creases on her forehead. Tears streaked my face and the world looked bright and blurry. But her face was clear. And close.

Isabella stood for everything uncertain and unstable and risky, and yet as my mind threatened to reel back in frantic circles, I found stillness in her dark eyes. I held onto that stillness for dear life.

Just then a spatter of rain tickled my face, cooler than my tears. Isabella let go of me and held up her bare arms to feel the drops. She looked off to the west where dark clouds gathered. "Oh, no. There's a storm coming."

White-Breasted Nuthatch
(*Sitta carolinensis*)

"I wonder if we have time to get back before it starts . . ."

She didn't wonder for long. As we turned to walk back to the boat, a downpour hit, drenching us instantly. My dress clung to my skin and my hair hung limp down my back, stringy and dripping. I didn't care. It jolted me out of my confusion and flipped the mood like the toss of a coin, and for that I was grateful.

The storm erupted so suddenly that Isabella and I laughed as we plodded through the mud and splashed in puddles like children. Gradually, the rain washed the ache out of my chest and I almost forgot about the woodpeckers. When we reached the familiar cove, I helped Isabella turn the boat upside down and hoist one end up high onto a boulder. Once the water drained out, we climbed underneath and let the boat shelter us from the rain. We shared our picnic lunch there, even though it, along with my shoes and stockings and hat, had gotten a little soggy. The simple meal tasted delicious after our romp in the rain. The few thick slices of dark bread, the hunk of cheese, the handful of ripe strawberries, and the tiny flask full of lemonade hit the spot.

"No gin?" I asked warily, eyeing the flask.

"No gin. All out right now."

"Where do you get it, anyway?"

"From Jimmy, in the band."

"Haven't you ever heard of Prohibition?"

"Are you kidding me? I think my mother *invented* Prohibition. Which is precisely why I choose to ignore it." She paused and then went on. "I used to be worse. I had a really bad job awhile back, and I needed the alcohol to help me get through the night."

Rain pounded down on the boat over our heads in a loud rhythm. I looked at her with searching eyes, wanting and *not* wanting her to go on. She shook her head, choosing not to elaborate. She changed the subject instead.

"What happened back there, Garnet? Why didn't you want to cut out those birds?"

I took a moment to think about it. Why was it, exactly? How could I make Isabella understand, when I didn't even really understand? The silence stretched out while I thought about how to answer her.

"I guess I couldn't see them for themselves—all I could see was that they were a mated pair, feeding and nesting together, raising babies and sending them off into the world. I don't think birds feel *happiness* exactly, at least not like we do, but they seemed happy to me anyway. Settled and content.

So watching them made me think about Father and about the fact that my family isn't really like that family of birds at all. And they made me think about Teddy, and wonder if I could have a happy family with him . . . or not."

I looked over at Isabella—those perfect lips, that short hair starting to dry with little tufts sticking up at funny angles, those boyish clothes all rumpled and soaked. I wanted to tell her secrets I hadn't even told myself yet.

"There's so much waiting for me at home, Isabella. Eventually this summer will end and I'll have to go back. August twenty-sixth is branded in my memory like judgment day. There are decisions to be made, big decisions. See, the thing is I . . . I can't end up like my mother," I said, surprising myself with the sudden clarity of my desires. "I can't marry Teddy and have children and call that a life. The woodpeckers are happy with that, but I don't think I could be. I want to learn. And work. And see things, and do things, and be somebody."

"I know, Garnet." The patter of rain filled the small silence between us. She pressed her small hand onto my knee, and underneath the wet and nearly transparent fabric of my skirt, my clammy skin warmed instantly at her touch.

"Can I tell you a secret, and you won't tell anyone?" Isabella said.

"Of course."

"My name's not Isabella."

I laughed. "It's not? What is it?"

"Mary Elizabeth."

I laughed until my stomach was sore, and she joined

me. Laughter filled the tiny space under the boat until we were wrapped in the sound, safe in our own little world.

Then our eyes caught, and held, and her lips came closer. And closer. Until they were on mine and she was kissing me and I was kissing her back.

I was a hawk on the wind.

After a split-second eternity, her laugh made me pull away.

But it wasn't coming from her. No, the source of the sound was outside our boat cave. It was the birdsong I'd been trying for so long to place, the soft, single-toned, whistle-like *whi-whi-whi-whi-whi-whi-whi*. I had to know. I peeked out under the rim and peered through the rain. There, climbing head down around a tree trunk just beyond the clearing, was a simple little gray-and-white bird. It pecked at the bark of the tree, sheltered from the rain by foliage, and there was no mistaking it.

"A nuthatch?" I said when my tingling lips remembered how to speak. "I never would have thought . . . not an exotic species at all! Just a plain, common . . ."

"What?"

I looked at her—really looked—and all at once the nuthatch made sense. This girl next to me was only part Isabella, the stunning scarlet tanager. She was also part Mary Elizabeth, the simple nuthatch. So what was I, then? Part Garnet, the boring American robin, or the ordinary ring-billed gull, or the drab little chipping sparrow—but maybe part something else.

"Mary Elizabeth," I whispered.

"Seriously, Garnet," she said, clearing her throat. "Will

you still call me Isabella? I was never very good at being a Mary Elizabeth."

Her face was close again. So close. The air hung thick and humid around us, in our under-the-boat world.

"I'll call you Isabella. Whenever I'm not calling you beautiful. Or amazing. Or—"

She kissed me again and my words were lost. I was drowning, and I'd never been more grateful in my whole life.

"I have another secret," she said, pulling away. I waited, anxious to take back her lips again. "I wrote to my brother. I sent him mail-order boxing gloves. I told him to follow his dream." My heart swelled up and I kissed her again and again and again.

The rain let up some after awhile, and I reluctantly asked Isabella if we could head back. It was getting late and I was worried I'd be missed at the hotel.

"I don't know . . . I suppose the rain isn't all that dangerous. There hasn't been any lightning, I don't think. We'd get soaked again, but I think we'd make it back all right."

"Let's go then. It's getting late and I really don't want to get caught."

I helped her flip the boat and carry it into the water. I tossed my shoes in and swung myself up into the dinghy. She climbed halfway in and pushed us off with one leg. Once she was settled, we were off. The boat wobbled in the choppy water and Isabella struggled with the oars, but luckily the wind blew at our backs, so despite the rough water we slowly moved toward the mainland.

When we were well away from the island but still

far from the docks, thunder cracked through the air like a horseman's whip. Lightning followed, streaking from sky to land not a mile away.

Isabella's eyes stared in panic. "Come sit beside me," she called, her voice distorted by wind and fear. I scrambled over to her bench. She spoke straight into my ear so the wind wouldn't whisk her words away. Her voice stayed calm, but with her side touching mine I could feel her trembling. "Take this oar and *pull*. We have to get to land, fast."

"Is this—dangerous?"

"Metal boat, flat lake," she said. "Yes, it's dangerous."

The image flashed unbidden into my mind—a newspaper clipping with a photo of my body, washed up on the shore, limbs tangled around the half-dressed corpse of the beautiful dancehall girl and a headline reading "Family Shamed by Young Woman's Fatal Act of Indiscretion." As if capsizing and drowning weren't enough to fear, I was suddenly paralyzed by the risk of getting caught. My parents accepted Aunt Rachel, but she was a grown woman and not their daughter. What would they think if they knew about the things I'd done with Isabella?

"Garnet, *help!*" Isabella shouted.

I pulled my oar with both hands, splinters digging into my soft palms. Thunder rumbled all around me and lightning split through the clouds and down to earth. The oar whooshed through the waves; the hinge creaked as I hauled the oar out of the water and back toward the front of the boat; the oar splashed back into the white caps.

Isabella's rowing was much smoother, and although she

matched her pace to mine, her strokes were more powerful and the boat listed. We were pointed far off course now, and I thought about giving up and hiding in the bottom of the boat while Isabella fought the waves alone. She'd be better off without me. When she looked over at me, I thought she'd tell me to go back to the other bench and let her do it.

"Switch sides with me," she said instead. "I'll get us back on course."

I slid down the bench as she got up and resettled on my other side. I labored with that oar for a while. The thunder crashed louder and the lightning flashed closer and closer, but the dock inched closer too. The bottom of the boat disappeared in ankle-deep water—rainwater, and lake water that was splashing up as waves threw themselves into the sides of the boat.

We switched sides three more times, sloshing into our new positions, and by then my arms burned from the strain. My fingers, white and wrinkled from the water, cramped up from gripping the oars and ached with chill. Goosebumps covered my arms and I blinked away the water that ran down my face and into my eyes. Gradually, we crawled nearer to the land.

At last, we pulled up alongside the dock and scrambled out of the boat. Isabella hastily wound the rope around the post and we bolted for shore.

"We made it!" she cried as we finally felt solid ground beneath our feet.

"I have to get back, but thank you for today. Thank you." She squeezed my hand. Hard. I could feel her meaning.

"Good luck," she said, turning and running for the picnic pavilion.

I knew I'd need it.

When I crept up to the hotel, a group of people was gathered on the north end of the veranda. Mrs. Harrington's unmistakable shape was among them. They stood looking out at the huge maple tree—one large limb had been severed by lightning and lay on the grass just a few feet from the building. It must've been a close call. I couldn't sneak around to the back door with them looking out like that, so while they gawked I slipped past them through the front doors. My heart fluttered with the knowledge that if just one of them turned I would be caught.

Avery saw me and started to say something—I must've been frightful looking—but I put my finger to my lips to shush him. He nodded and opened the door for me in silence, and then shut it quickly behind me. I raced for the stairs. I needed fresh clothes, a hairbrush, and a good lie, *fast*. Today, I was up to the challenge.

Unfortunately, so was Hannah.

"My, my, don't you look a mess," she said, looking up from the settee in the sitting room as I entered the suite.

I opened my mouth but nothing came out.

"No need to invent something. I know exactly what you've been up to."

European Starling
(*Sturnus vulgaris*)

"I sent Charlotte to fetch you at the library when we heard on the radio that a nasty storm was blowing in. She said you weren't there—the woman at the desk told Charlotte she hadn't seen you today."

"Hannah, I—"

"I saw you with her, Garnet. That harlot from the dance hall. I looked out and saw you in that boat with her out on the bay."

I'd been so worried about getting to shore safely that I hadn't even realized how visible we were out there—in the only boat on the water during the storm. So she knew where I'd been and whom I'd been with. Not good.

But then there was the deeper fear: had I done anything, anything at all, that would make Hannah guess what had happened between me and Isabella? I thought back. No. I hadn't kissed her or held her on the dock. She'd just held my hand. The good-bye had been harmless enough. We'd been under the boat on the island, hidden from the world, when the rest had happened. My heart fluttered, remembering, and heat rose into my cheeks.

"She's my friend, Hannah. I met her at the hat shop a few weeks ago, and we've spent some time together since then. Her name is Isabella. She's a wonderful person and she's become quite a good friend to me. Please don't tell?"

"I don't know . . . I can't imagine what Mother would think if she knew you were spending time with that, that wild girl. The job is one thing, but you really shouldn't be socializing with such a common, low-class"—her voice dropped to a whisper—"slut."

The words stung. I could hardly believe the cruelty in them. How could she be so harsh, so unfeeling? "Oh, Hannah, please? Isn't there anything I can do for you in return for some discretion on your part?"

The girl's pointed face lost all its malice then, and I was taken aback by how quickly she could shift her look from mean-spirited sharpness to simple seriousness. Clearly she wanted to negotiate—this was her aim from the beginning. But what could she want from me?

"Yes. There is something you could do." She looked up, and she allowed her face to soften further, into what almost looked like pleading. "I need help, Garnet. With schoolwork."

I sat down next to her, stunned. I didn't even know Hannah *had* schoolwork to do. "What do you mean?"

"I don't . . . read well. And my math and science are atrocious too, but that doesn't worry me so much. It's the reading, see." Tears came into her eyes then, and she blotted at them with the corner of a perfectly embroidered handkerchief. She looked sincere, and yet she was clearly watching my reactions and tailoring her performance to get what she wanted from me.

"Go on," I said, kindly, eager to take the bait. "Tell me."

"Mother doesn't think it's all that important. I'm good at the music and painting and needlework and all those things, and she thinks that's enough to make a good match, but I'm afraid that no one will want to marry a . . . a . . . simpleton." All cunning went out of her at that word. She burst into genuine tears and buried her face in the hanky.

"Oh, Hannah," I said, reaching out to pat her back and trying to hide my bewildered expression. "I'm sure it will all work out fine."

"That's not all," she said after blowing her nose. She looked at me with honest-to-God fear shading her face. "We're not actually very rich. Not anymore."

I blinked, no longer able to hide my astonishment. I'd guessed that they were living beyond their means, but Hannah's expression told me the situation was more dire than that.

"It's all credit. All of it. We still own the estate, but Mother refuses to live on what the land actually brings in, for fear of looking poor. So we're dreadfully in debt. She's expecting what little we still have invested to keep growing, and she's got a plan to develop some land in Florida, but mostly she's just hoping that I'll marry well and save us all from ruin."

Hannah's shoulders hunched under this burden as she

spoke of it. Mine seemed so light in comparison—I was expected to marry Teddy, and the match would bring joy and comfort to my family, but the decision ultimately changed little other than my own future. After a moment Hannah went on. "What Mother doesn't realize is that men today want more than just a pretty doily maker. I can't rely on my flute or my paintbrush to win a husband. I need to be smart. Interesting. I need to be able to read. My tutors have given up, and Mother told them not to bother about it."

"I'll help in any way I can, Hannah. I promise. We can start today if you want. All I've got are bird books, but they'd be as good as anything I suppose."

"Yes. Okay, thank you. And I won't tell about the dancing girl if you don't tell Mother that I've said all this. She won't mind that you're trying to teach me—even though she'll think it's silly, she won't stop us—but she would mind tremendously if she knew I'd blabbed about the money trouble."

"Deal."

She looked nervous but grateful.

"Let me clean up first, and then we'll begin."

In my room, I sat on the bed a moment and tried to figure out what had just happened. Who was this girl, Hannah Harrington? I didn't know her at all. I'd dismissed her as an irritating mama's girl, when really she was both a conniving manipulator and a fearful child with very real troubles. I still did not like her. In fact, her wicked insults to Isabella and the revelation of the true depths of her cunning made me dislike her even more than before. But at least now there was an interesting complexity to her character and her situation. And now, like it or not, we were allies of a sort.

Then the exciting truth dawned on me: with Hannah in on the secret, I could see Isabella as often as I wished. I penned a note to her immediately: "Off from work tomorrow—can I meet you first thing in the morning? I will come to your place if you tell me where to find you. It's safer now. Love, Garnet."

Then I picked up the bird book with the most illustrations and rejoined my cousin in the sitting room. The book fell open to the European starling, a common little blackbird known for the way its plumage changes from black with white spots to an oily rainbow of green and purple during breeding season. I laughed. Do we all change when we try to attract a lover? Do we all try to be more beautiful, or more bold, or more intelligent, or just more brilliantly ourselves?

"What's funny?"

"Nothing, nothing. Okay, show me how much you can read on your own."

I had no idea how to teach reading, but I was more than willing to give it a go, both for Hannah's sake, and for my own.

Northern Oriole
(Icterus galbula)

"Pick one," Isabella said. "Anything you want. My treat."

But there were so many choices, too many choices.

The rolls and sweet buns and cookies stood like soldiers, lined up in the case in neat rows. The air in the shop was warm from the ovens and hung thick with cinnamon. I stood with Isabella in the middle of the bright, clean bakery, gaping like a child at the loaves of fresh bread heaped in baskets along the sidewall and the gleaming pastry cases filled with treats.

A man in an apron dusted with flour crashed through the swinging door with a tray of fresh croissants balanced on one hand. The buttery little crescent moons shone golden beneath their snow of powdered sugar. My choice was made. I turned my pleading eyes to Isabella and she nodded. "Done," she said.

"She'd like one of those please," she called to the

man, who had begun to arrange them on a platter on the counter. He looked up at her, his eyes softening with recognition as they landed on her pretty face. Then he looked to me.

"A croissant for the young lady," he said kindly, choosing one with a thick coating of sugar and tucking it into a paper bag.

"No, make that two," she said, winking at me. "Two."

Isabella paid with coins from her beaded purse, and we settled on a bench outside the bakery to eat. We watched people going about their morning business while we savored the flaky rolls that made our fingers greasy and left crumbs on our laps. Some of the townspeople nodded to Isabella as they walked past us, and some saw her and looked away quickly, hurrying past, not bothering to hide their disapproval. Everyone, friendly or unfriendly, seemed to know her. And yet not one of them approached her as a friend.

I'd excused myself after Sunday breakfast in the dining room, telling Mrs. Harrington I was off to wander the town for the morning. "My legs need a good stretch," I'd said. Hannah cast me a knowing look as I left but I knew she'd keep her word. I made my way to Isabella's apartment, which was situated above the bakery on Main Street. Following the directions on her note, I climbed the back stairway and knocked at number four. As I waited for her to answer, I wondered what was behind that door. What would her apartment look like—a young woman living alone? Then she bustled out the door and closed it behind her, not giving me a chance to find out, and I didn't want to snoop. Another time.

Since she'd worked late the night before and was slow getting started that morning, she suggested we pop down to the bakery for a treat before heading out. So there we sat, presiding over Main Street and finishing off two warm croissants.

"Your note said, 'It's safer now.' Whatever did you mean by that? Did Mrs. Harrington die or something?"

"No, no." I crumpled the empty bag in my hands and I told her, in hushed tones, about my conversation with Hannah.

"Well, how's that for a juicy bit of drama!" She licked the crumbs off her lips.

"She called you some terrible names."

"Oh, never mind about that. Hannah Harrington can call me whatever she wishes. And if these people want to snub me," she gestured into the street and called out, "so be it!"

"It must be marvelous. I mean, how wonderful not to care what anyone thinks of you."

"But I *do* care, don't you see? The uptight people are *supposed* to think I'm a threat, just like the crowd at the dance hall is supposed to think I'm . . ."

"Beautiful? And carefree and youthful and—sexy?"

"Yes. See? It's all about what people think of me. Sometimes, to tell you the truth, I lose track of myself under all the makeup and the glittery costumes. It's an act. I love the dancing, but the rest of it kind of wears me out. That's why I like to be with you."

She must've seen the question in my eyes. I'd been wondering for ages why she enjoyed my company.

"With you," she said, "I know who I am. Or at least, I know who I want to be."

I couldn't kiss her there, in the middle of town, so we sat in silence a moment as the grocer across the street watered his flowerpots and a group of vacationers passed us, chattering, on the sidewalk.

"Would you like to see the dance hall in the daytime?"

"Oh, please take me," I said, leaping up.

I tossed the bag in the trash can next to the bench as Isabella brushed crumbs from her skirt. Then she stood up and offered me her arm, like a gentleman would offer his arm to a lady. I giggled, took it, and marched off down Main Street at her side.

If people gawked, *so be it!*

The dance hall was dark and ghostly during the day. Our footsteps echoed as we walked through the empty space, and a musty smell of dust and sweat lingered in the air. When Isabella spoke, she whispered, as though we were in a church.

"Would you like to see my dressing room?"

I nodded. I followed her through a door to the side of the stage and down a dark hallway. She pushed open a door at the end and motioned me inside.

Racks and racks of bright costumes stood against the walls of the close little cubby. Hats rested on head-shaped stands that stood on high shelves, and a mess of makeup covered the top of a scratched-up vanity at the far end. Mirrors bounced all the colors back, making the tiny room seem twice as vibrant as it was, and twice as crammed.

"What do you think?" Isabella asked, her voice returning to its normal tone. She picked a filmy scarf up off the floor and hung it on a hook behind the door.

"It's fabulous. It's just like the show was that night: bright and loud and dazzling." I ran my hand along the rack of fringed and beaded costumes.

"Do you want to try one on? Here, how about this?" She pulled a black and orange one off the rack and held it up. It was shimmery and bold, like an oriole's stunning feathered breast, and it would seem ridiculous on me.

"Oh, I couldn't," I said, feeling heat jump to my face.

"Why not?"

"That's a dress for an oriole, Isabella, not a sparrow like me."

As soon as I said it, I remembered the nuthatch. I remembered Mary Elizabeth. And I wondered—

"Oh, come on, just put it on."

Then her hands were on me, lifting up my dress. I inhaled sharply, surprised, embarrassed, realizing too late that I'd scared her off. Her hands were gone.

"No, I couldn't," I said, flustered, as I resettled my dress. "But there's one thing I would like."

"Anything," she said.

"Could I stand up on the stage?"

"Of course," she laughed. "Come with me."

She led me out of the dressing room, down the hall, up three steps, and through a different door.

"And now," she said in a booming voice through the open door, "the act you've all been waiting for—the lovely, the talented, the legendary, Garnet Richardson!"

With a little push, she had me through the door and out on the platform. I took three small steps forward, and just stood there. I looked back to Isabella and she nodded. With three more steps I was in the middle of the stage, where I stopped to look out over a sea of imaginary people. All of their imaginary eyes were on me. And what did they see? That was the question. I had no desire to perform, but there was a burning wish in me to be *seen*. I wanted someone to look at me the way I looked at birds—without thinking they knew what they'd find, without trying to fit me into a mold they'd already formed in their head.

When I turned back to Isabella, *she* was looking at me that way. If she could, and if *I* could, maybe that was enough for now. I had her for only another six weeks, and six weeks suddenly seemed like no time at all.

I jumped off the stage and Isabella and I headed toward the park, together.

"The ori-ole is common in open deci-decidu-deciduous wood-lands or am-among scattered small trees."

"Hannah, you're doing wonderfully. Why on earth did you think you couldn't read?"

"This book is a lot simpler than what my tutors have used. The pictures help me figure it out, and there isn't too much text at a time. Since my teachers think I should be proficient by now, they've been pushing all kinds of impossible books at me—Greek philosophy and Old English poetry."

"Do you read your mother's magazines? The newspaper?" After I said it I realized I knew the answer. I hadn't seen her pick up a magazine or newspaper all summer.

She blushed. "Sometimes," she said, "but I'm just, you know, intimidated. Since I'm not very good."

"We'll practice, Hannah, with easy books at first. Then you won't be so scared. Now, go on. You were reading about the northern oriole."

Mourning Dove
(*Zenaida macroura*)

"It's charming, Isabella."

"Well, I cleaned . . . a little."

I ran my hand over a fringed curtain that rippled scarlet under my fingers. The apartment was small, with a tiny kitchen and bathroom and living space, a door to a single bedroom, and a narrow window overlooking Main Street. The carpets were dingy and the paint chipped, but she had covered as much of the place as she could with costume fabrics and dance hall posters. It was perfect. It was all hers.

"Would you like a tour?" she said, laughing. We could see the whole apartment from where we stood.

It was a Sunday evening, the first of August. Two wonderful weeks had passed since the day we'd visited the dance hall together, and with my arrangement with Hannah working out so well, I felt it was safe for me to spend some time at Isabella's apartment. Isabella didn't have shows on Sundays, and the Harringtons were out for the evening at another lady's summer cottage on the other side of the bay, so tonight we were free to spend some real time together. Alone.

After my "tour," we settled on the little sofa in the living room. Within moments, the mood turned melancholy. In three and a half weeks I'd be going home, and our impending separation colored everything we did together now.

"How about a record?" Isabella asked.

Music seemed like a great idea.

"Sure."

"King Oliver?"

"Is that jazz?"

"Of course, what else?" She leapt toward the cabinet in the corner. It was a well-worn record player; she touched it lovingly. She fished the King Oliver record from a disorderly pile and pulled it out of its folder. The motion was almost like a knight drawing a sword from its scabbard. Jazz was Isabella's weapon—with it she fended off all the monsters the world threw at her. The monstrous thought of August twenty-sixth was definitely something to combat with jazz. She carefully set the record on the turntable and flicked the "on" switch. It hummed and then popped and crackled as she lowered the arm. Then the room filled with the scratchy swing and swell of King Oliver's Orchestra.

A grin leapt to Isabella's face and she started to shimmy and shake as though King Oliver himself was using her as a marionette. She kicked and twisted and stepped and stomped freely, impulsively, like it was more natural for her to dance than to stand still. I perched awkwardly on her sofa and watched.

"Dance with me, darling," she said, beckoning me over with a flutter of her fingers.

I stood but hung back, timid, feeling the weight of my lanky arms and legs anchoring me to the floor. Isabella looked like she could take off at any moment, but I didn't know how to shake off my clunkiness. I wanted to learn; suddenly I desperately wanted to learn, and this was my chance to learn from *her*. I might never get another. "Will you teach me to Charleston?"

"Come here, girl."

I moved toward her, biting my lip.

"Like this," she said. "Follow me."

I tried to copy her movements, but mine came out awkward and jerky. We kept at it—step, kick, step, step, step, kick—until we were doing as much laughing as dancing. Then she threw in variations: thigh slaps, foot slaps, hip slaps, trotting, jumping, knee holds . . . She taught me to scooter and to charge, to do the coffee grinder and the Suzie Q, all in the tiny space of her sitting room. Gradually my limbs freed up and the rhythm found its way into my heartbeat.

"Keep with it, Garnet. You're doing great," Isabella panted after four or five songs, smiling at me. We jiggled and jived, laughing with tears in the corners of our eyes. The little apartment shook with the sheer joy of it, like it was about to fall apart, but I wasn't worried. At that moment, I felt ready for anything. And if the building crumbled to the ground, the two of us would've lifted up into the air and danced away.

When the record ended, Isabella put on some Louis Armstrong and we collapsed onto the sofa. The raspy, throaty voice and the smooth cornet seeped into our lungs and our veins and the world's turning slowed down. He was a mourning dove, with that soulful call. We were spent, exhausted, and the wild joy of the dancing settled into a quiet calmness. I was afraid that the lightness would leave me if I stopped moving, that the worry and the melancholy would sink back in, but they didn't. Even in rest, I could feel that the dancing had changed me—the lightness was part of my bones. I traced the leaves that twisted up the faded upholstery of Isabella's sofa with one finger, imagining the Louis Armstrong dove gently crooning from the brush as it foraged for seeds. Isabella hummed along to the music with her head resting on the back of the sofa and her eyes shut.

As one song melted into another, we drifted closer together till we were holding each other on the sofa. The sun had set, and as darkness spread out over the street outside the lamps were lit one by one. There wasn't much to say, so we just held each other. Then the energy between us shifted, just slightly, and the holding became touching. We kissed silently as the room grew dark. What happened then surprised me, but didn't. She pulled my dress up and up and over my head. With deft fingers she unlaced my camisole and I didn't stop her as she removed every stitch of my underclothes. I was exposed.

In my sudden nakedness I glanced nervously at the door and then the open window. All was quiet—no one would disturb us. When I turned back, Isabella's dress was gone and her slip was halfway off, her pale skin like powdered sugar sifting out of it as she worked it over her head. I caught my breath at the sight of her. No going back. My hands were on her then, before the slip had even fallen to the floor. All hesitation evaporated into the hot summer air and we became a moving tangle of arms and legs and hands and lips. It was a slow, silent carousel ride, and I gave in completely to the dizziness.

Afterward, we dressed and cuddled up together as the spinning world settled back into calmness. Isabella fell into a soft sleep, and I found my scissors on the end table and snipped out her silhouette. It was the first one I'd done of a person, but I just pretended she was a bird and found her borders. I'd traced them often enough with my hands and my eyes that the lines of her face were familiar to me. She slept peacefully, and her stillness made it easy for me to capture the subtleties of her high cheekbones and full lips. Sure enough, the finished cutout looked just like her. On the back, in white chalk, I wrote, "Never forget who you are."

Did I know who she was? I knew a lot, but not everything. There were things she never talked about, and I'd never pressed her for them. I'd almost forgotten about the gaps in her history, too intrigued by what she did tell me to worry about what she didn't. But her practiced hands on my skin reminded me of the things she didn't say, and now I had to wonder: who had she been with before me? She'd been my first, but I was obviously not hers. *Harlot*, Hannah had called her. Could the rumors be true?

"I don't care," I whispered to her sleeping form. "I love you." Then I left the cutout on the coffee table and slipped out of the apartment and into the night.

I crept in through the kitchen door of the Galpin—I had no idea how late I was or if I'd be in trouble. The kitchen was safer. A cook was chopping vegetables for the next day's meals as I came in, and someone was washing dishes amid a cloud of steam, but the kitchen was pretty quiet at this time of night. Avery leaned against a counter, talking softly to a young colored woman whose face I couldn't see. He saw me and smiled.

"Are they back yet?" I asked.

"No, I haven't seen them."

Then she turned. It was Charlotte. I gasped.

"Don't worry, Miss Garnet," she laughed. "If my mistress finds out about all this, it won't be from me." She shook her head and looked at Avery. "The things that woman doesn't know . . ."

"Thank you," I said with a sigh. "I'll go up then."

"Anything you need?" Avery asked.

I shook my head and moved toward the lobby. They went back to their whispered conversation.

Sure enough, the suite was empty when I let myself in. I was safely in bed by the time the Harringtons returned, and dreaming of mourning doves.

Great Blue Heron
(*Ardea herodias*)

"Garnet, come here, listen to this," Hannah called. The book I'd given her to study lay open in her lap, her finger resting on the place she'd left off reading. We'd been working together three weeks, and although silent letters and diphthongs still tripped her up, she did pretty well as long as she had some context for what she was reading and some interest in it. I'd offered to find her books on an interest of *hers*, but she seemed reluctant to give up the bird books when she was just starting to get comfortable with them, and I didn't want to push her.

When I abandoned my letter to Alice and moved down the veranda to join Hannah, her finger tracked up the page a bit and then resumed its travels across the words she thought might interest me. Her halting voice read the passage aloud:

Crane Island is situated in the upper portion of
upper Lake Minnetonka, and has received its name
from the circumstance of its being the breeding
and roosting place of the "Blue Cranes" as this species is popularly called. How long it has been thus
occupied is not even traditional, for it was a heronry earlier than the Indian traditions began . . .

"Keep reading, Hannah. You're doing wonderfully. I
can't believe there is a heronry here—right *here*—and I didn't
even know it. Read me some more."

"You take a turn, Garnet. My eyes are starting to cross."
She passed me the book and pointed to where I should
begin. I continued:

Early in the mornings, between the 5th of May
and the 20th of October, they may be seen flying far away in all directions till all have departed.
Then from four in the afternoon until dark, the
birds return . . .

I took a moment to skim over the herons' mating ritu-
als and nesting habits, forgetting Hannah's reading lesson
entirely in my excitement. A little farther down the page, I
began to read aloud again:

Since that lake has become a great summer resort,
and is constantly plied with steamers, yachts,
and row-boats constantly flitting back and forth
at all hours of the day and night, it is a standing

surprise that these birds (and their copartners, the cormorants) still continue to return year after year to the same familiar spot. However, it must be confessed that from these disturbing causes, to which should be added a long-continued practice of firing pistols at them from the steamers' decks to see the females rise in clouds from their nests, and the robbing of their eggs by men and boys by the employment of telegraph pole climbing irons to reach them, their numbers became so sensibly reduced as to call in special legislation, or all would have been destroyed or driven entirely away.

"Blue cranes . . ." I said, gazing out toward the lake and absentmindedly handing the book back to Hannah. "'Special legislation' means they've passed laws to protect them—that means they might still be out there! When was this published? Must have been during the time of the great steamers with that reference in there. Look in the front of the book for the copyright information."

Hannah pawed through the first few pages, searching for a publication date as I'd taught her to do. "I think, yes, 1892," she said.

"Quite awhile ago. Well . . . the heronry *might* still be there. If it is, I must go. And I must bring Miss Maple. She has to see it—see what it is that thoughtless people can so easily destroy."

My love for Isabella and my productive truce with Hannah had combined to give me a blissful happiness that had lasted weeks. But it was imperfect happiness, because

it was marred by two things: first, my impending departure for home and all that awaited me there, and second,
my disappointment in myself for not pursuing the feather
issue with Miss Maple. A trip to Crane Island just might
resolve our disagreement and clear my mind of that second
impediment to joy. The fact that it was Friday, the sixth
of August, was beyond anyone's control, but Miss Maple's
ornithological education was clearly my duty. If I fancied
myself a concerned scientist, and not just a hobby bird-
watcher, there was no time like the present to take some
responsibility and begin to act for change.

Over the weekend, I did my research and set the whole
thing up. Our departure on the *Stillwater* streetcar boat was
set for five o'clock, and since Mondays were notoriously
slow in the park and we'd doubtless be the only passengers, I'd talked the captain into letting us drift awhile at the
heronry.

"You don't want Crane Island, though," he said. "In
1906 a storm blew most of the trees down on Crane Island.
The herons' old territory was turned into a summer cottage
retreat in 1907. But the birds still roost on Wawatasso, the
next-door island, even though speedboats swarm the lake in
the summertime and picnickers are constantly invading their
territory. It's amazing, really, that they've held out."

"Can you take us there?"

"Why not," he said with a shrug. "Monday at five.
Don't be late."

When Monday dawned, I told Mrs. Harrington the
truth about where I'd be for the afternoon and evening—

but would Miss Maple agree to come? As soon as I arrived at work, I proposed an excursion to my boss.

"I'll stay the afternoon today and help you close up, Miss Maple, if you'll come out with me after work. There's something I'm dying to show you."

"How mysterious," she said with a sly grin. "Sure, why not. Business is so slow on Mondays, but you can help me tidy the back room if you like."

We spent the afternoon filing papers and organizing boxes and making small talk. After closing up shop at half past four, I led Miss Maple down to the docks. We were indeed the only passengers, and we had our choice of seats. We claimed a bench near the prow on the main deck, a little ways behind the captain. Responding to the deafening shriek of the steam whistle and two clangs of the captain's bell, the dockhands untied the moorings and the engineer fired up the hissing steam engine. The boat backed away from the dock and then meandered toward the upper portion of the lake and into Smithtown Bay.

It was a heavy, humid sort of day, so once the trip was underway, we climbed the steep steps to the upper deck to lean on the painted railing and feel the cool lake breeze. We watched the water part beneath us and felt the wind on our faces as we chatted. We'd been talking the better part of the day, and the conversation now began to range freely into more personal realms. Before I knew it, I was telling her I was thinking about going to college instead of getting married right away.

"What about you, Miss Maple? How come you never married?" I ventured to ask.

"Well, unlike most spinsters, I made a choice to stay unwed. My parents died when I was about your age, and everyone told me I had better find myself a husband. But I had this crazy dream about running a shop, so I took my meager inheritance and started a business with it. I'm married to that hat shop, I suppose." She laughed, and the reflection of the water danced in her eyes.

"You support yourself."

"Yes. It can be done."

"You do what you love."

She patted my hand where it rested on the railing. "Life is too short to do anything else."

The captain's bell clanged once and the steam engine's whirring slowed to a stop. We drifted just offshore of a beautiful, lush little island. My heart jumped. "This is Wawatasso Island," I told Miss Maple. "This is what I wanted you to see."

She looked at me suspiciously, and then gazed out toward the bit of land before us.

The island was a tiny untamed wilderness scattered with elms and sugar maples, covered with dense underbrush, and bordered by rocky shorelines. The whole island was dotted with majestic blue-gray herons, and more swooped down every moment, flying home from a long day of hunting. In flight, they folded their elegant necks, stretched their legs straight out behind them, and flapped their huge wings in slow, powerful movements against the deep blue sky.

The magnificent creatures filled the air, the shoreline, and the trees, and I could barely breathe for the splendor of it. Just like the blue baby Aunt Rachel caught all those years ago, I was shocked breathless by the beauty of life. I took out my scissors but I couldn't cut. I knew I could never capture the scene before me—a hundred birds fishing and flying and roosting together. No wonder the book spoke of Crane Island in awe as a miraculous triumph of conservation over thoughtless destruction. The site had moved but the vision was still glorious.

I looked down for a moment to catch my breath, and there on the water was the boat's shadow, and my own. With the early evening sun behind us, we cast a dark outline on the still water of the bay. There I was, a lanky shade perched atop the boat next to Miss Maple's plump form.

I looked closely at my edges, my boundaries, the slightly elongated lines that set me apart from lake and sky and island and bird and boat. I looked closely, pretending that I knew nothing about the girl I saw, pretending that she was some beautiful creature whose borders contained something worth holding in—something unique and extraordinary, something worth saving. I looked closely, the way I'd taught myself to look at birds, the way I'd learned to look at Isabella, and I saw *myself*. Then those scissors were cutting after all, as I snipped out my own image. I ignored the small ripples of the water and traced the lines that separated me from the world, and the lines that fit me into that world like the piece of a puzzle.

Yes, my father was falling apart at home and my mother was trying to put him back together. Yes, the girl I loved was rehearsing with a band for an evening show in a dance hall that some people loved and many people loathed. Yes, the boy I was supposed to marry was eagerly awaiting my return home with a question on his lips. Yes, Mrs. Harrington and her daughter were back at the hotel wasting their lives tatting lace and lying about money. And yes, I was a part of it all. But I was also separate. I had my own life to live, and no one but me could live it.

I took a deep breath and looked up at Miss Maple, who was still staring, mystified, at the view.

"So what do you think?" I asked. "Look like a bunch of nice hats-to-be?"

Her jaw dropped. She turned to me, offended, appalled. "Never again," she said, her shoulders squared, her eyes full of the resolution. "Maybe it will hurt business, but I don't care. Never again."

With those words, and the knowledge that I'd brought them out of her, I knew that college would be the right decision. The more I learned, the more I could do to change people's minds, to open their hearts, to be an active force in the world and in my own life too.

Clang. The decisive tone of the captain's bell cut through my thoughts.

The boat's engine started back up and our shadow moved on the water. We continued the tour of the lake, and Wawatasso Island and its inhabitants slipped away behind us. *Someday,* I thought, *maybe I'll come back here to study these birds.* I imagined my student self drifting at the island for hours on end, taking photographs and scribbling notes and sketching images and even making sound recordings. Could I get permission to land on the island officially and investigate the nests? Has anyone done a census of this population recently? Might I someday write about these incredible birds and the measures taken to protect them? Or give a lecture? Or set up an exhibit in town to inform people, to educate them? I smiled out over the water at the thought of it all as more and more birds passed overhead, winging steadily toward the island. Going home.

"You know," Miss Maple said later, as we walked back toward town from the docks, "I have a sister in Minneapolis. She's a telephone operator. It's part-time work and it pays pretty well. Let me know if you ever need a job and I'll see if she can figure something out for you. Might help you with that college plan."

"Thank you," I said, my voice shaking just a little. College *plan*. Not a *dream* anymore, but a *plan*. The thought frightened me, but it felt right too, and telling Miss Maple made it so much more real. Would I be able to make it happen? Even with a part-time job to help with the cost I would still need my parents' support, and that, I knew, would be a hard thing to come by. I would just have to figure it out. I was determined.

I hugged Miss Maple good-bye for the first time in our short relationship, and we parted ways.

When I got back to the hotel, Avery had a letter for me. From Mother.

Dear Garnet,
This will come as a shock to you, and I would like to deliver the news in person, but I will not be able to make it out to get you until the end of the week. I told you your father was improving, but

I'll confess that I exaggerated—out of hope, and a desire to protect you. The truth is that his condition has, if anything, deteriorated over the last two months. He lost his job, and instead of looking for another he turned to drink. Before I realized how desperate he'd become, our savings were gone. And now, I must tell you a truly horrible thing. Your father has left us. He boarded a train for the West Coast last night while I was sleeping. He left a note saying that he no longer wants to trouble his beloved wife and daughter with his terrible sadness now that he can no longer even support us. He fears that the war will never leave him, and so he felt compelled to leave us. I had hoped it would not come to this. I'm sure you're well aware of the fact that I sent you away in part because I thought that time alone with him might help me bring him around. But it was not to be.

You are a young woman now, and so you must understand that this puts us in a precarious position. I will need your help in supporting our small family now that we are without a proper breadwinner. I know that Teddy Hopkins has intentions to propose to you, and I urge you to consider this option. Please do not allow your parents' failed marriage to discourage you from settling down. Teddy is a good boy, and he would make a fine husband to you. There is also a chance that you could graduate early and secure a teaching position. We both know that I am not educated enough to get a very good job.

I will come out to Excelsior on the Friday afternoon streetcar, after I have wrapped up some business here, and stay with you there for a few days so we can talk all this over. Then we can make the journey home together.

Take care, my dear daughter, and be strong. I will be with you shortly.

Much love,
Mother

I read it four times. Then I went into my room and closed the drapes and did not come out. I didn't eat or sleep, and all night long I didn't even cry.

All that time I thought and thought. I thought about Father—gone. Gone. He'd been a ghost for so long already that it surprised me how sad I was at the thought of him actually being absent from my life, my home. In truth, it was the *hope* that was newly gone. The hope that he would someday get better, return to us, forget the war, and really live again. Take me back out into the woods and point out deer tracks again. Chide me for walking too loudly, grab my arm to guide me over a downed tree, teach me to mimic birdcalls with whistles and hoots.

I thought about Father, but I also thought about myself. And I could not think of a way out. My mother needed me. I had to go home. And marry. Or find full-time work. I could not be so selfish as to think about going to the university, or running away with Isabella, or suggesting that Mother move in with Aunt Rachel or with her parents on the farm. There was no way out. And I didn't even have until August twenty-sixth anymore. Mother was coming on Friday. Friday the thirteenth. What an ominous date for the end of my trip to fall on.

I lay on my bed, in all of my boating clothes, staring at the ceiling and letting my brain turn in circles around the dilemma. No way out.

At dawn I pulled all the silhouettes off of the wall over my bed and ripped them to shreds. I stuffed the whole mess into the trash basket. I pulled the one I'd just done of myself out of my pocket and destroyed it too.

And that was when I began to cry.

Common Loon
(*Gavia immer*)

I stayed in the hotel suite until Friday came. How could I see Isabella? What would I tell her? *It's over. I'm going home to marry a boy I don't love so I can support my mother and myself without quitting high school to find work.* I desperately didn't want to have to say those words to Isabella. She, the daring girl who had left her home and family at age fifteen to forge her way in the world as a dancer, would never understand. She'd made her decision, and now I'd made mine too. There was no other way. So I hid there, and Charlotte brought me my meals. The Harringtons knew what had happened to my family and they stayed out of my way, either out of pity or because the scandal embarrassed them. I didn't care which.

Finally, on Friday morning, I ventured down to the veranda. Mother would be arriving that afternoon and I needed to pull myself together. But my nerves were still raw and every word out of Mrs. Harrington's mouth grated on them like old chalk on a blackboard.

I sat down with Hannah and opened the daily paper. "Want to read this with me?" I asked halfheartedly. "Have you been practicing?" She nodded, clearly hesitant to upset me, and turned her eyes to the paper.

"I don't know why you're wasting your time with that, Hannah dear."

"I want to better myself, Mother."

"Yes, yes. So you've said." She chuckled and returned to her Sears Roebuck. We carried on with our reading.

"Start here, Hannah. This story looks interesting." She began:

"Our Trudy Swims Channel"
Gertrude Ederle courageously struggled against the tide for three hours before her triumphant fin-ish on the French shore at ten o'clock Wednesday night. Our Trudy, the first woman to swim the English Channel, beat the male record by almost two hours. Is there nothing the new American woman can't do?

I stared at her picture, Trudy's picture, there on the front page of the *Minneapolis Star*. She was sleek in her black bathing costume and swimming cap, like a seal. No, like a loon, that graceful diving waterbird of the north. Her bare arms hung, exhausted, from her broad shoulders, but there was a look of incredible strength in her eyes, as though she now knew for sure that she could not be conquered.

"Must you read that rubbish?" Mrs. Harrington said, interrupting my thoughts and Hannah's reading. She reached over and snatched the paper away. "Can you believe any woman would allow men to take photos of her in such a revealing bathing costume?"

"I certainly wouldn't," Hannah giggled obediently.

"Good," her mother said with a nod. "No shame, I tell you. No shame."

"I think she's amazing," I said under my breath. "Here, Hannah, let's read this." I opened my bird book to a picture of a loon. A proud bird, a powerful bird. A swift swimmer with a haunting call that raised goose bumps on the arms of anyone within earshot. Hannah read, and I tried to focus on the description of the bird, its fishing techniques, nesting habits, its migration patterns, but I kept looking back to the photo of the animal, with its steady eye and confident posture. And my mind kept roaming back to Trudy and the English Channel. Her strength. I grew restless and squirmed in my seat.

"Now this," Mrs. Harrington exclaimed, jabbing her finger at the catalog in her lap, "*this* is a proper bathing costume. Look here, Hannah, isn't it lovely? Simply divine! Pretty but modest and just a little bit elegant. I must order you one. It would look gorgeous on you. You may need two, in fact, since they make them in all different colors now. Would you like that, dear? Shall I buy you two?"

As Hannah listened to her mother I could hear her breath coming out in little bursts. Her hands clenched into fists. Then she stood up suddenly, jostling me, and the book we'd been sharing fell to the floor with a *thump*.

"I don't need two!" Hannah hurled the words at Mrs. Harrington.

"What on earth has gotten into you? Child, do sit down and stop talking crazy. You're making a scene."

"I will *not* sit down and I am *not* crazy. *You* are crazy. Why do you do this? Pretend we are so rich when all our money's gone? You keep spending and spending so that no one will find out our secret, and it's me who's going to have to sell my life to pay for it all. It's cruel and deceitful and . . . and positively shameful, Mother."

It poured out of her in a jumble of bitter words. Mrs. Harrington just stared at her daughter in shock afterward as the girl puffed with anger. I was so proud of her, standing up for herself like that, and without thinking I rose from my seat and took her hand.

"Let it out, Hannah. You've held all this inside so long."

"How do *you* know about all this? Who told you?" she whispered, her dagger eyes moving from her daughter and pointing at me. "Was it Charlotte? I'll send her away if it was her."

"It wasn't Charlotte, Mother. It was me," Hannah growled, slapping my hand away. I hadn't meant to let on that she'd told me—I should've acted surprised. It couldn't matter now, could it? Since Hannah had blurted the truth out to the world, I was sure she wouldn't care that her mother knew she'd already told me.

But I was wrong. "I'm done with secrets, done with lies," she said, her words sharp as razors. "Do you want to know what Garnet's been up to this summer?"

Our fragile pact broken, Hannah spilled out the truth

about Isabella. Or most of the truth. Thankfully there were still intimate details that she didn't know and couldn't tell. She told about my lies, my sneaking off, my adventures on the town and in the park with "that common harlot from the dance hall, that little slut with the drinking problem and the tiny dresses."

"How could you associate with such riffraff?" Mrs. Harrington gasped. Then her voice dropped and an ugly sneer spread over her mouth. "First the business with Rachel, then your father, and now this, as if your family needs another scandal! I will be telling your mother about your behavior, young lady."

"Fine. Tell her. It doesn't matter anymore. Nothing matters anymore."

And then I was out the door and running, running to the lake. Heartache and anger poured down my face in tears as I ran until I could hardly see where I was going. Then I stood at the shoreline, in the little inlet that would never host a summerhouse for Mrs. Harrington. I stared out at the hypnotic waves until my sobs mellowed into sniffles and hiccups. I reached down and took off my shoes, dipping my bare toes into the cool, clear water. That coolness jolted me awake, and I knew I had to feel it against all of my skin. Like Trudy, like the loon. Trudy was strong enough to make her way in the world of men. But there were all kinds of strength. If she had to make sacrifices for her family, to leave behind anything and anyone who tempted her away, wouldn't she do it?

I looked right, and left. No one. Once I was sure I was alone in the secluded cove, I pulled my dress over my head and tossed it on a rock. My underclothes would serve as an even more scandalous bathing costume than Trudy's, but with no one there to disapprove, I didn't care. The breeze tickled my bare arms and legs.

I crept slowly into the water, letting the coolness inch up my body and pull my mind into my skin. I shivered and strode out farther as the water climbed to my knees, then my waist, then my chest. I took a deep breath and allowed my legs to buckle under me.

The water lapped against my chin and I felt suddenly light, as though the lake cradled me, rocked me in cool watery arms. Water pressed against my skin and my skin pressed back against the water and the boundary was, in that moment, so wonderfully defined. I was myself because I wasn't sky or water or sand. Where I stopped, the lake began, and I began where it stopped. The water opened up a space for me and held me close. *This is who you are*, the lake said to me, speaking through my skin. Just like a dark bird against a clear sky, just like a sleek black loon against glimmering waves, I had a silhouette. I'd thrown away the one I cut of myself at the island, because my dream for what I could be had gone up in smoke when Mother's letter arrived. But now I had to retrace myself, fit myself into a different shape. I could do that, couldn't I? I could be the shape of a young lady, a beautiful bride, a wife, a mother, a good daughter. That was the shape I needed to be now. And maybe life was just a matter of putting on the right costume moment to moment, and smiling for your audience.

I squeezed my eyes shut, took a deep breath, and

dunked. The world I knew disappeared. There was a moment of close, silent darkness, and then I emerged, sputtering into the daylight. It was a rebirth, I told myself. Now I was ready to do what I had to do—to meet Mother at the station and tell her yes, of course, I would help us survive without Father. I would put aside all those selfish desires, leave Isabella, and go home to Teddy and to the rest of my life.

I almost had myself convinced.

And then I heard a voice call my name like a rock shattering glass:

"Garnet!"

It was Isabella, standing on the beach, pulling her shoes off, stripping down to her underclothes without a moment's hesitation. *No! No, no, no. Not now.* She ran into the water with splashes of her pale legs and ducked under the waves. Before I knew it she was right there, on me, her slick wet limbs entwined with mine as she tried, playfully, to drag me under the water.

Every kiss and embrace we'd ever shared came flooding back to me. My very skin rebelled as I forced myself to pull out of her grip. *It's for the best*, I thought.

"Where on earth have you been?" she said. "I've been looking for you for days. You haven't been to work, or to town, or to the park . . . I didn't dare go to the hotel. Avery said something was wrong, but he didn't know what." She turned serious then. "There's, um, something I need to tell you. Something important."

"No, I have to say something first." My voice cracked. Where had all that strength and sureness gone? "I'm . . . I'm leaving. Going home."

She looked at me. Blinked. "What? When?"

"My mother is coming on the streetcar today. She's taking me home on Sunday."

"Why? I thought you still had some time before school started."

"Something's happened. My father, he's—he's left us."

"Oh, Garnet, I'm so sorry."

She reached for me and I flinched away. I knew that her touch would weaken my resolve.

"I'm going home and getting m-m-married."

Her look turned in an instant from sympathy to incredulity. "But—"

"I have to. My mother can't support us on her own. And I want to finish high school and graduate with my class. We need a breadwinner—and quickly—so I have to marry. And Teddy, well, he's a good man. He'll take care of us. He can start working his father's business while he finishes school. We'll get by."

"I can't believe you. What about the birds, Garnet? What about college?"

"I can't, Isabella." I had to make her stop asking those questions, those painful questions. The pain turned to meanness and I could feel it building in me, needing an enemy, needing to spit the pain back at someone. At her. "I'm not like you. I have an obligation to my family and I'm going to honor it."

That stung her. She turned from me. "Fine. Throw your life away."

Tears mixed with the lake water on my skin, and

underneath it all the meanness boiled. "I have to do this. I don't expect you to understand. And I have to leave you now."

"But I had something to tell you."

I was firm—ice in my eyes and hot lava behind them, just waiting to spew out. Whatever she wanted to tell me, I didn't want to know. I was done with her. Done. "Mother will be here soon and I need some fresh clothes before I go pick her up. I can't see you again."

"You hypocrite. You coward." She threw the words over her bare, trembling shoulder and they hit me like blows. Coward? But I was being strong, doing what I had to do. What did Isabella know about obligation, responsibility? She just threw out rules when they didn't suit her, and threw out people when they got in her way. Even family. Family! My fury built up until I couldn't help but hurl it at her, all the pain and meanness erupting. It came out in Hannah's voice.

"At least I'm not a common harlot," I said.

And I hated myself instantly.

She turned to me slowly; her smudged scarlet tanager lips fell open in shock at my cruelty. Other people's insults she could shrug off, but from me those words sunk in deep. "Do you know where that rumor comes from? No? Well, I'll tell you. The job I worked before this one didn't mind a bit that I was underage as long as I was willing to leave my dressing-room door open after the show and let men in— any man who paid the manager the price. I was supposed to *entertain* them, and I did, even though some nights I had to swallow a fair amount of gin first. Tough job, huh? But I did it. *I'm* no coward. I was willing to do anything so that

I could dance onstage. Anything. So I guess that makes me a *common harlot* and not fit to associate with a *fine lady* like yourself. And that's fine with me. Just fine. So go," she said. I didn't move. Lead had filled my bones and I was so heavy. "Go!"

I turned, the sand under my feet suddenly feeling rough, and sloshed back to shore. I threw my dress over my wet underclothes and picked up my shoes in one hand. I trudged off, barefoot, forcing myself not to look back.

Eastern Screech Owl
(*Otus asio*)

That night Mother slept beside me in the small bed. She'd been so relieved and grateful to hear of my decision, so proud of me for putting my family first. Mrs. Harrington told her about Isabella, using the most alarming language she could find, claiming that even though we were "no longer family," she would hate to see me bring my mother disgrace. But Mother was so pleased with me for deciding to marry that once I assured her the friendship was over she didn't bring it up again. Her approval felt warm and comfortable and affectionate and safe, and it was reassuring to go to sleep with her close-by. I hadn't slept next to her since I was a child, since those lonely nights when Father was first away at war, and I'd forgotten just how soothing it was to have her near.

But my dreams were anything but soothing. I dreamed of Isabella. She wore the oriole dress even though she wasn't working. It was night, and the park glowed like a sparkler with dancing, spinning lights. Isabella pulled me through the whirling mess of rides, laughing that nuthatch laugh of hers, and lured me onto the roller coaster. I'd made a point of staying off that frightful contraption all summer, but now somehow Isabella strapped me in beside her and I couldn't move. We lurched forward and then her laugh became a shriek. The sound was light and joyful in the beginning, and so close it could have been coming from my own mouth as we climbed the first hill. Then we paused at the top and my heart stopped beating for what felt like an eternity while we waited for the plunge. Finally, we inched over the precipice and the world dropped away beneath me. Isabella's close, happy shriek became a scream, and when I looked over, she was gone, and a gray-and-white-patterned screech owl perched on the bar where her hands had rested a moment before. The small, stocky owl looked at me with yellow eyes and then lifted up on its great wings and silently flew off. In the distance, I heard it calling in that descending whinny that gave it its name. The roller coaster vanished, and I was looking for her, trying to follow the muffled screeching that was so filled with pain and fear. The lights swirled around me as I stumbled aimlessly into the night.

Mother shook me awake.

"Fire, Garnet. Wake up. Fire!"

I opened my eyes into even deeper darkness than the sleep I'd left behind.

But this darkness was heavy and filled my lungs. Stung my eyes.

I coughed.

"Come on," Mother said. She grabbed the sleeve of my nightdress and yanked me out of bed, then fell to her knees and pulled me down with her. The air near the floor was clearer.

Muffled screams came through the darkness. Not bird-calls but human screams. Flames rumbled somewhere far off. Glass shattered. Wood splintered in some other world.

Here, near the floor, it was quiet.

"Wait," I said, coughing. I reached up and grabbed the blue jay handkerchief from the night table. I ripped it in two and dunked both halves in my water glass. "Your mouth," I said, handing one to Mother.

She felt for it in the dark and took it. With the wet cloth over my mouth and nose I could breathe a little easier. "The door's here," I said through the cloth as I crawled like a three-legged dog across the floor. Mother followed; I could feel her close behind me.

I traced the route through the small bedroom by memory, and when we reached the door, I knelt and put my hand up to grope for the knob.

"Ah!" I cried. The metal burned like a skillet.

"Oh, Garnet," Mother murmured. "It's too close. I hope the Harringtons got out. Can we go another way?"

I clutched my hand to my chest. It screamed. I tried to think over the throbbing of my skin. "Yes." I scrambled back toward the bed and past it. Toward the dimly glowing rectangle on the opposite wall.

"The window?" she said when we reached it. "But we're too far up."

"No. The veranda. Trust me." The drapes were

already pulled back and the window was open—even mother slept immodestly in the August heat. I stood up and stuck my head out into the night. The air was clearer there and my lungs sucked it in. I bunched up my nightdress and hauled one leg over the sill, and then the other. My feet hit hot shingles. Hot, but not skillet hot. The roof of the veranda. I turned and helped Mother out.

Here, the sounds weren't as muffled by smoke. The screams were close. The flames were close. The breaking building cried out with pops and cracks and moans. I led Mother to the edge.

"It's too far down," she said. And it was. Farther than I'd thought. Fifteen feet? Twenty? I'd forgotten about the staircase down from the veranda to the ground. We were nearly two stories up, not one. But there wasn't any other way.

"We have to," I said.

"They'll come for us. The firemen."

"We can't wait."

"They'll come," she insisted.

"No, I have an idea." I sat down on the hot shingles and reached with my feet, swinging right and left. Then, yes! They hit wood. The support column. We could *climb* down. I turned to motion for Mother to come.

Then, with a sudden *pop*, the roof we perched on tilted dangerously. I gripped the edge with my knees and my hands, the burned one sending a wave of pain up my arm. Mother dropped to all fours and clung to the shingles like a cat in a tree.

"It's under us," she said.

We couldn't climb down—we'd be climbing *into* the blaze.

"We have to jump," I told her.

"They'll come," she said.

"I'll go first."

She looked at me with wide eyes for one, long moment. Then she inched toward me. At my side, she gripped my arm and met my eyes. She nodded once. "Courage, Garnet," she said.

My father's voice echoed in my head: *Fly, Gigi, fly!*

I looked down, and down, and down. The ground stretched out safe and solid beneath me, but I knew its solidness might kill me. And if I had the courage to jump out of a burning building, I also had the courage to speak the truth. If I was going to die in the next minute, there was something I had to say to my mother first.

"I can't marry Teddy, Mother," I said into her panicked eyes. "I need to go to college."

Then I jumped.

Northern Cardinal
(*Cardinalis cardinalis*)

I jumped—and I *flew*.

In my white cotton nightdress I hovered there, suspended above the panic and pain, the chaos and confusion. The whole scene paused for a single moment and my desperate childhood wish for flight was granted. I felt the wind against my skin and turned my eyes to the stars. The brightest ones burned calmly through the smoke and the wavering heat.

In that moment I knew that wanting was not the same as selfishness. Wanting was pure and right and beautiful. And the real me could not change shape to suit the needs of others—not even loved ones, not even family. I knew who I was. The rest could be worked out. I could find a way. If Miss Maple had done it, so could I.

And then, I crashed to the ground. The pain came rushing in with a breathless jolt. My knee burned, and a stabbing ache pierced my shoulder. Every inch of me was on fire, like the hotel on fire, threatening to collapse.

Mother appeared beside me then. She must have followed me out into the night air. I didn't see her jump, but there she was. She clutched her ankle, but her relief seemed to overpower the pain. She took me in her arms and we lay there, on the ground, rocking each other amid the panicked crowd.

It might have been mere minutes later that I regained rational consciousness, but it felt like hours. Mrs. Harrington's voice cut through the bustle.

"Well, go in and get them," she was shouting to a fireman.

"Ma'am, I'm sorry, but your finery is not our first priority."

She gaped at him, appalled. "Young man, those dresses and hats and jewels are worth more than your annual salary—more than *twice* your annual salary, I should think—so march in there and retrieve them. Room 209—"

But the young man in question was gone, off helping an old woman that another fireman had just carried from the blaze.

"Do I have to do *everything* myself?" Mrs. Harrington said in a huff, heading toward the burning building.

"No, Mother, don't!" Hannah cried. "It's not worth it!"

"Not worth it?" Her voice lowered then, but I could hear her still as she lectured her daughter. "It's all we have, Hannah. You know that—you told everybody all about it this morning. What do you want, the poorhouse? Do you want us to have to sell the estate? We'll never get you a husband without at least the trappings of wealth. The credit's run out. Lord help us, Hannah, it's all we have."

Hannah Harrington turned her furious face to her mother and aimed one pointy finger at the huge woman's chest.

"It is *not* all we have, Mother. We have each other, don't we? If you go in there and that building collapses, *then* we'll have nothing—or at least *I'll* have nothing. No finery and no husband *and* no mother. If that's what you want, fine. Go."

The finger pointed to the blaze.

The singed woman stood staring at her furious child for a long moment, her own anger turning ever so slowly to incredulity. The whole scene around us seemed to pause, to hold its breath.

"What's gotten into you today?" Mrs. Harrington said sharply, but then her scolding tone shifted, softened. "You're not my little girl. You're a young woman. A fierce, beautiful young woman. What on earth am I going to do with you?" Then she gathered Hannah up in her enormous arms and sobbed.

As if someone took a piece of charcoal and decided at that moment to redraw her, Hannah's hard angles all melted. I watched, and finally I saw the two of them for what they were: a pair of people facing the world together, trying to do right by one another without losing themselves in the process. Just like me. Just like all of us.

"Garnet, you're shaking." Mother rocked me in her arms as the firemen and medics rushed around us in a blur of frantic activity. A bright red fire truck blared its two-note siren like a cardinal gone mad. "We have to get away from here," she said. She coughed and clutched her ankle. "But where? Where can we go?"

"I know a place," I said, trying out my knee and finding it functional. "Can you walk?"

I knocked, sheepishly, on the door of Isabella's apartment. After I'd yelled at her and called her names and made her cry, here I was, knocking on her door in the middle of the night, asking for a place to stay.

At least I hadn't brought the Harringtons. They'd vanished in the bustle and we'd decided to go without them. We needed to find shelter quickly, and we trusted they'd find someplace to go too. And as Mrs. Harrington had so graciously pointed out, we were "no longer family." In any case, I was grateful to be spared their company at this moment as I waited for Isabella to answer her door, hoping that she'd let us in, dreading that she'd shut us out. She had every right to turn me away.

At last, she answered. Isabella, in a slip and smudged eye makeup and the detested night gloves. She stood there, her irritation at being woken up turning to surprise and then concern at the sight of us.

And she opened the door wide for me—for grimy, battered me and for my injured mother.

We stumbled inside. Isabella slept on the sofa and gave us her bed. Mother and I dropped into that narrow bed and slept instantly. Deeply. Side by side.

. . .

I didn't wake up fully until Sunday. It was late afternoon when I sat up in Isabella's bed, groggy and disoriented. Mother still slept, so I tiptoed out of the bedroom and shut the door quietly behind me. The apartment was empty, but I found a note from Isabella on the kitchen counter. *Gone to rehearsal and then a show—manager scheduled one last minute on my day off, bastard. Back late. Help yourself to a bath and anything you can find in the icebox and the pantry. Left fresh clothes out on the sofa—should fit. Isabella*

My stomach let out a vicious growl. I opened the pantry door and then stopped—my hands were stained black with soot. The bath would have to come first.

In the tiny bathroom I ran hot water into the cracked claw-foot bathtub and stripped off my once-white nightdress. I found a washcloth in the cabinet and a bar of soap on the edge of the tub. I lowered myself into the bath slowly, catching my breath at the sting of the water on little cuts and scratches I didn't realize were there. Heat welled up from my burned hand. Half an hour must have passed while I scrubbed at the soot and soaked the sore spots. The water soothed the ache in my knee while I rubbed my stiff shoulder. My head buzzed the whole time . . . The fire. The roof. The words I'd said to Mother. The leap. Mother's ankle. Hannah and her mother embracing. Isabella opening her door. Opening, opening, opening her door.

Isabella in her slip, with mussed hair and sleep in her darkly smudged eyes, opening her door. And giving us her bed. She must've spent the whole of Saturday and most of Sunday creeping around her own apartment so that we could rest. Then she went to work and left a note to offer us everything she had: hot water and soap and food and clothes and a safe place to rest.

When the water was cold and murky, I got out and dried off. *Isabella's towel*, I thought, gently pressing the terry cloth against my inflamed skin. Then I rinsed out the washcloth and found a bowl to fill with hot water. After I dressed in a clean shift of Isabella's, I brought the bowl in to Mother.

She startled awake when I touched the warm cloth to her black-streaked face. "Shhh," I said. "Just cleaning you up a little."

"Garnet, where are we?" she said, confusion and pain wavering in her voice.

"A friend's, Mother. We're safe here. We can stay as long as we need to." I hoped that was true.

A look of recognition passed across Mother's face as she recalled what Mrs. Harrington had told her. "A friend? Do you mean . . . the flapper?"

"Yes, Mother. Her name is Isabella."

I waited to be scolded, lectured, reprimanded for my poor taste in friends, but she just lay there quietly a moment and then said, "Well, we should be very grateful to this Isabella, then, shouldn't we."

We were silent for a while as I scrubbed at Mother's face and hands. Then I took the bowl back to the washroom and assembled a little supper for us in the kitchen. When I brought the plate of bread and cheese and fruit into the bedroom, Mother was sitting up, leaning against the headboard. Her eyes were clearer. She looked more alert.

"About what you said, Garnet . . ." She coughed, her lungs still rattling with smoke. I waited while she recovered, wondering what she'd say next. My shoulders hunched up with nervous tension and the hurt one smarted. Finally she continued. "I guess we'll have to find a way to make it work. I'm just not sure how. So I thought—Teddy—I don't know."

"It's okay, Mother. Don't think about it now. We'll figure something out. Here, eat."

But *I* thought about it. As we demolished the meal—almost identical to the picnic food Isabella had brought to Big Island—I thought about Miss Maple, and about that sister in Minneapolis and that job at the telephone company. *Let me know if you ever need a job,* Miss Maple had said, *and I'll see if she can figure something out for you.* What if Mother and I both needed jobs? Something full time for her, and something part-time for me while I finished high school and went on to college. Could we make it then? Was it possible?

I waited up for Isabella that night. I paced until I was afraid I'd wake Mother with the creaking of my footsteps on the uneven floors. Then I sat on the sofa, nervously tracing the vines on the upholstery with one finger.

She *was* late. The world lay in deep, silent slumber when she turned the knob and opened the door and quietly shut it again behind her. She busied herself in the entryway a bit before emerging into the sitting room with her shoes in her hand. She looked tired, and then startled to see me awake.

"Isabella, I'm so sorry," I said feebly. "I don't know how to thank you . . ."

She just looked at me, her eyes hard and then soft, hard and then soft. She padded over to me in her bare feet and sat next to me on the sofa. She took my hand. "How could I turn you away?" she said at last. "I love you."

I swallowed hard to keep the tears back. "I know."

She squeezed my hand and I flinched.

"What?" she said.

"Nothing, it's just . . . burned. That hand."

"Oh, I'm sorry." She let go and reached for the other one instead. "Everyone's been talking about the fire. No deaths, but plenty of injuries and the hotel is nothing but rubble." Then the Harringtons must be okay, and Avery too. Isabella would have heard if something had happened to any of them. I knew I should try to find Hannah and her mother, but it could wait.

"How is your mother?" Isabella asked.

"She's all right. Coughing some, and I think her ankle might be sprained, but she's okay otherwise. She's asleep now."

"And you? Are you okay?"

Besides the twinge in my shoulder and the ache in my knee and the terrible throb of my burned hand and my shame at what I'd done to Isabella and my fear for the future—"I'm fine."

"Come into the bathroom with me. I need to get this makeup off. My skin hates me when I fall asleep with it on."

I followed her and stood in the doorframe of the tiny bathroom while she dabbed at her face with cotton puffs. Gradually, the pallor of her skin and the jet black brows and lashes and the scarlet lips subsided into less extreme beauty. And who was to say which one was the real Isabella? Could they both be real? How many faces can a person have?

"I told her no, Isabella."

"What?" She splashed water from the running faucet up onto her face and then blindly reached for a towel. I handed her a dry one from the rack and she pressed it to her skin.

"Just before we jumped. I said no, I couldn't marry Teddy. I'm sticking to it."

Her clean face emerged from the towel and bloomed into smiles. She was radiant even without all the paint. And when she looked at me like that, I felt radiant too.

When I finally climbed into bed with Mother, my mind was buzzing with plans and ideas, my heart burning with hope. I didn't drift into sleep until the first gray light of dawn filtered into the room, and the cardinals whistled their clear songs into the morning air.

Common Grackle
(*Quiscalus quiscula*)

The next day, Isabella and I stood silently in front of the burned-out hotel, like it was a grave. The shell of the building stood at odd angles, and inside the skeleton black and gray ashes, like feathers in disarray, lay ankle deep where chairs and beds and tables should have been. It reminded me of Father.

The winter after he came home from the war, Father hit a grackle with our new Model T Ford. We were going out for a drive after church, and I was excited because I didn't get to ride in the car very often. I was sprawled in the backseat, enjoying the bump and jostle of the journey, when suddenly Father let out a curse and slammed on the brakes. I threw my arms out to steady myself against the lurch of the car, and winced at the crunch of bones beneath the tires. Father pulled over and we all got out. A light snow dusted our wool coats. The little broken pile of black feathers lay there in the road. I leaned back against the cold metal of the closed car door, looking at the small sleek creature that had become nothing but an ink stain on the white snow.

Then rage gripped me and I turned to Father, blame searing my tongue. But before I could speak, he stepped out into the road and bent over the dead bird. He scooped it up in his gloved hands and looked at it—at this common bird that most would consider a pest—with tenderness, respect, regret in his eyes.

"Garnet, get the trowel out of the glove box," he told me. I went.

"The ground is frozen, Albert. We can't bury it," Mother said.

"We can try," he told her. "We owe it that."

Father dug the bird a shallow grave, wrenching chunks of frozen dirt out of the ground at the side of the road. He laid it inside, whispered something under his breath, and covered the blue-black body with bits of brittle earth. He heaped a little snow over the mound, and I set two sticks in a cross shape on the grave.

Father stood up and wiped the snow from the knees of his trousers. Large wet spots remained. In a dark, heavy voice, he said, "Never neglect the dead. The ones you've killed will haunt you, always."

He wasn't speaking to me.

Now, I stood with Isabella in front of the wrecked hotel, which was lying there in its rubble of soot and ash, and it looked just like Father's grackle had, that snowy day. And I thought of him. I had memories of him cupping a frog in his huge rough hands, him kissing Mother full on the lips. I knew he had been a living man once. His sadness had made him seem dead for so long, but with Mother's hopeful letters I'd almost started to believe he would come back to us. Now he was really gone, from me at least, and I found myself gazing up at the ruins of the hotel and saying good-bye to him. Wondering where he'd go. Wishing him luck.

Maybe he would find a new place to live, a new life, a new happiness. Or maybe he would wander, like the chimney swift who never perches anywhere for long.

Fly, Daddy, fly! I thought, imagining the dark shape of the swift darting through the sky. First the grackle, then the swift—my mind was full of dark birds as I took in the sight of the ruined building.

Isabella seemed pensive too. She shivered despite the heat and I stroked her hand.

"I tried to tell you that day, in the water . . ."

"What? What's wrong?"

"Mitch is sick."

"Oh, no."

"I got a letter from my mother. The boxing gloves arrived and so she finally had my address. She wrote to tell me Mitch has been ill for months now. They're not sure he'll make it."

"I'm so sorry."

"And I have a sister. Sophia. She was born a little while after I left—she's almost two now and my mother says she already likes to sing."

She swallowed hard and sniffed and a tear inched down her cheek, leaving a little trail of mascara. I turned to her and put my arms around her, pressing her into me. I didn't care an ounce if people saw.

"What if they break her of it? The singing?" she said into my shoulder. "Like they tried to keep me from dancing?"

"She's your sister, Isabella. I'm sure she'll be strong like you."

"I can't trust them to raise her right. And I have to see Mitch again before he—he—in case I can help make him better. I have to go home." She pulled away and looked at me with fear in her eyes.

"You can do it, Isabella. You had the courage to leave. You'll have the courage to go back."

"The season's almost up. My contract ends in September. I'll go then, and plan to stay the winter, and see what happens."

I smiled, wiped a tear from her cheek. It was possible that I'd never see her again, but even knowing that fact and letting its weight sit on my heart, I could never tell her not to go to her family.

"Do you want to go in?" I asked. "I think it's safe." She composed herself and nodded. We borrowed heavy shoes and thick gloves from two firemen who were just finishing the day's cleanup work and ventured inside.

We picked our way to the northeast corner of the wreckage, where three floors' worth of debris lay in one thick layer. The hem of my borrowed dress trailed in the deep ashes—I'd picked Isabella's longest skirt and it was actually a little *too* long for me, but otherwise her clothes fit me pretty well. I liked having the smell of her close to me all day long.

I didn't know what I was looking for, pawing through charred bits of unrecognizable furniture and the broken porcelain of bathroom fixtures. There was nothing left. I didn't mind; it almost made it easier to start over, for me and Mother, and for the Harringtons too. For all of us, maybe. I saw a piece of a lantern, and a tune found its way into my head. I began to hum, and then to sing quietly under my breath:

> *But should the surges rise, and rest delay to come,*
> *Blest be the tempest, kind the storm,*
> *Which drives us nearer home,*
> *Blest be the tempest, kind the storm,*
> *Which drives us nearer home.*

After awhile I called to Isabella, "We can go now. Are you ready?" She nodded solemnly. I looked around me one last time. Then I led Isabella out, not the quick way straight through the gap in the crumbled wall, but through the front door and down the broken staircase that had once been so grand. A proper good-bye.

"We have one stop to make on our way home," she said as we emerged. "You need a new pair of scissors."

When we reached the stairs to Isabella's apartment half an hour later, she took them with decisive steps: up, up, and up.

I scrambled after her and grabbed her before she

reached the top. From one step below her, I held her close, pressed her against me, buried my face in her shoulder. My injuries had mostly healed but mother was not walking on her ankle yet, and I did not fear discovery. Isabella lifted my chin with one hand, the other gripping the railing so we wouldn't fall, and kissed me, hard. Once, twice, three times, again and again.

I lost count of kisses and minutes and up and down and pain and joy and fear and loss and happiness and risk. I'd say that there was nothing in the world except her right then, but that would be a lie. There was *everything*, and it filled me up to bursting.

Mallard

(*Anas platyrhynchos*)

As we washed up from breakfast the following morning, a knock at the door startled us. I shut the door of the icebox and shot Isabella a puzzled look. She stood at the sink, up to her elbows in suds.

"No idea," she said. "Can you answer it?"

I wiped my hands on a dishrag and hurried to the door. It swung open to reveal Hannah Harrington. She wore a green linen shift and her hair was tied up simply. Under her arm she carried a thick book. She looked older, calmer, more composed.

But when she spoke, she stuttered. "I—I have your book. I was up reading it that night, so I had it with me when the . . . well, here it is."

"Oh, Hannah, come in, come in. It's a library book, but thank you for bringing it. I'm so glad to see you well."

She came through the doorway followed by Avery,

who I hadn't seen standing behind her on the stairs. "He was kind enough to show me where he thought you'd be staying," Hannah said in explanation. She glanced shyly around her, and then looked at her feet as Isabella came into the entryway.

Isabella dried her hands and rushed to embrace Avery. "Everyone told me you made it out of the fire okay," she said, "but I had no idea where you were."

Hannah and I stood back, or tried to, in the tiny space. "Let's all of us go for a walk," I said. "There's so much to say and I could use some air."

I excused myself and found Mother in the sitting room. She sat in a chair by the window with her injured leg propped up and a pair of Isabella's pants in her lap. *If you don't give me something to do, I'll go mad,* she'd said to Isabella that morning. We had phoned Aunt Rachel (who I knew would always be *Aunt Rachel,* with or without Father around) to ask her to send us a few things, but they hadn't arrived yet, and Mother was stir-crazy without any work in her hands. Reluctantly, Isabella offered up her pile of mending. At first, Mother looked appalled by the pants, the sleeveless blouses, the short dresses, but she collected herself after a moment and said *Of course, dear. It's the least I can do.* Now she was happily at work.

"Who's here, Garnet?" she said, her needle continuing its neat progress along the seam as she spoke.

"Hannah Harrington and the doorman from the Galpin."

"Oh, good. The girl's all right, then. Do ask after her mother." Under her breath she added, "Even if they aren't exactly relations anymore, we ought to be civil."

I told her we'd be out walking for a bit but I'd be sure to pass along any news. In a moment, we were out the door and headed for the lake.

At the Commons, Isabella and Avery walked along the shore a ways while Hannah and I found a bench overlooking the water. A mother mallard bobbed in the shallows, tipping her tail up as she searched for food under the waves. Half a dozen of her almost-grown children milled about her, mimicking her movements as they refined the skill. They'd grown to be almost the size of adult ducks, but their feathers still stood out in some places when the wind blew. A few months ago they were nothing but puffballs lined up behind their mama, but now it was mid-August. Soon they'd have to fend for themselves.

"We're staying with the Pedersons at their summer cottage until we take the train home next week. They sent their driver to fetch us as soon as they saw the fire across the bay that night and realized it was our hotel. We couldn't find you or your mother, but people told us you were okay."

"It was all confusion that night—thank heaven we all made it out. So you're headed home soon then."

"Yes. And do you want to hear some crazy news? Charlotte said she wouldn't come without Avery! It turns out they've had a romance going all summer and none of us knew it."

I looked at her in surprise. "I guess none of us was paying any attention," I said. "I certainly wasn't." I had considered him my friend, but all I'd really done was use him. I'd needed him but offered him nothing of myself, and I was so caught up in my own story, I'd never even asked about his. *You'd be amazed how self-involved people can be,* Isabella had said once. I felt ashamed of myself, suddenly, but happy for him.

I looked down the shore to Avery. He seemed to be telling the very same news to Isabella at that moment because she laughed and grabbed his arms and danced him around in a circle, hooting.

"So Charlotte threatened to stay here in Minnesota if we didn't offer Avery a job," Hannah was saying. "Mother said she couldn't spare her after all these years, so Father would just have to find the boy some work with one of his buddies from the country club. We can't afford to employ him ourselves, of course. They're going to marry at the city hall before we leave."

He'll be stuck with Mrs. Harrington forever, I mused. *The things we do for love.*

"Avery wanted Isabella to stand up with him at the city hall next week," Hannah went on, "and I asked him to bring me along when he asked her, so I could see you and—and apologize."

"You don't need to apologize, Hannah."

"Yes. I do. I'm sorry I called her those awful names. She's—um—it's very generous of her to take you and your mother in like this."

I nodded. "We're leaving in a few days. As soon as Mother can walk on her ankle."

"What then?"

"Oh, who knows? I'm going to finish school and apply

to the university. Mother's going to look for a job, and I'll probably find something for the weekends too."

I must've looked nervous because she said, "I'm sure it will work out."

"Thanks. And good luck with, you know, the eligible young men of St. Louis."

She giggled. "Yeah, maybe that will work out too."

"You look lovely, by the way. That green is stunning on you."

"Borrowed. But yes, I rather like it too. The Pedersons' daughter has got me reading fashion magazines now. I might be done letting Mother pick my clothes."

"They always mean well, but they don't always know best," I said.

The mallard in the bay tipped too far forward and her legs kicked comically in the air as she tried to right herself. She finally surfaced and shook herself from her beak to her tail, water droplets flying. The young ducks watched her, then went back to their meal.

We laughed and laughed.

EPILOGUE
American Goldfinch
(*Carduelis tristis*)

The morning we left Excelsior, Isabella came to the station to see us off. When the streetcar swung up to the platform and yawned open its door, I hugged Isabella briefly and kissed her cheek. Mother did the same and I heard her whisper a thank-you in Isabella's ear. Then, as Mother hobbled toward the car, Isabella handed me a package wrapped in brown paper.

"Don't open it until you're on your way," she said. Then she squeezed my shoulder and hesitated a long, painful moment before stepping back. My skin already ached for her, but I steeled myself with a deep breath and turned away. We boarded the streetcar, dropped our tokens into the fare box, and claimed a bench seat. As we sped out down the track, Isabella's waving form disappeared behind us.

Mother pulled an embroidery hoop out of the traveling case Aunt Rachel had sent and began stitching hearts on a handkerchief. I chuckled. Aunt Rachel had thought of everything. I turned over Isabella's package and carefully removed the paper.

And there, in my lap, lay a sequined dress with black fringe—just like the oriole dress, but yellow. A goldfinch dress. *My* goldfinch dress, apparently. I blinked away the tears that gathered in my eyes. On a note pinned to the dress, Isabella had written, "You are no sparrow. I hope you know that now, my bright, beautiful Garnet. Have courage and you will *fly*."

I will, I thought, as we soared across the landscape—toward home, and school, and the one life that was mine to live. *I will*.

AFTERWORD
AND ACKNOWLEDGMENTS
Fact and Fiction in Silhouette of a Sparrow

Readers should know that Excelsior, Minnesota, is a real town; Lake Minnetonka is a real lake; and there really was an Excelsior Amusement Park in that town and on that lake that ran from 1925–1975. I grew up in Excelsior, but I was not born until 1982, and so the stories of the amusement park have always fascinated me in a way that only something just missed can.

I've tried to paint an accurate picture of the area, the town, the Commons, the amusement park, the lake, and the historical era of the 1920s, while inventing characters and situations within those settings, and while giving the story room to grow beyond the facts. Many details from the text are true: a man who ran the carousel for years did indeed start collecting fares at the single red light so he'd know if anyone was trying to sneak on; the *Minnehaha*, along with other steamers (or streetcar boats), was sunk off of Big Island in the summer of 1926 because it was considered outdated (it has since been hauled up from the bottom of the lake and restored); the great blue herons did move their roosting place from Crane Island to nearby Wawatasso Island because of a storm, and Crane Island then became yet another vacation spot. Countless other details are either true or as true as local legend can make them, while some facts were fudged for the sake of fiction. The Galpin House of the story is a fictitious blend of the real Galpin House and other hotels that served vacationers in that area during the 1920s. (A photo of the Sampson House that I kept by my desk most directly inspired the architecture of the story's hotel.) The fire of this story is fictional, but hotel fires were very common in those days and many Lake Minnetonka hotels burned and were rebuilt during that era. The twisting tunnel ride really existed, but was part of the park's Fun House, which was not built until the '50s. The hat shop is a locale of my own invention, but a feasible addition to the town's Main Street, while the bakery and its upstairs apartments are real. The Excelo Bakery was a favorite haunt of my childhood, and a friend of mine lived above it for a time, but the beloved shop has recently closed, along with the town's hardware store and drugstore. Like all small towns, Excelsior is ever changing.

A word must be said about Garnet's precious birds. I am no ornithology expert, but I wrote this novel with one hand on my Sibley bird book and one eye out the window. The birds mentioned here are all found in Minnesota, are all given their correct Latin names, and are all described with their real habits and habitats in mind. Any errors in the text come out of my own well-meaning ignorance, and I beg the birds' and the birders' forgiveness for any inaccuracies. The passage discovered by Hannah about Crane Island is adapted from a real book: *Notes on the Birds of Minnesota* by Dr. P. L. Hatch, published in 1892. As I wrote, Garnet's passion became my passion, and she gave me the chance to learn so much about these amazing creatures, as well as to learn about the constant struggle in the modern world between conservation and destruction—between conscientiousness and thoughtlessness. It is an issue very close to my heart and one vital to our future on this beautiful planet.

I owe many thanks to the Excelsior-Lake Minnetonka Historical Society staff and publications, the Minnesota Streetcar Museum volunteers, the special collections librarians at the Minneapolis Central Library, and many other patient and generous people who helped me delve into the history of this area. Thank you to my editor at Milkweed for believing in my vision for the book and for helping me make it a reality. Thank you to my writing group for years of insights, patience, and emotional support. And finally I must thank my parents for raising me in such an inspiring town, my advisors at Hamline University for helping me craft this story (draft after draft), and my partner, Emer, for giving me the courage to write and rewrite it (day after day).

MOLLY BETH GRIFFIN is a graduate of Hamline University's MFA program in writing for children and a teacher at the Loft Literary Center. She is the author of a picture book, *Loon Baby*. *Silhouette of a Sparrow* is her first young adult novel. She lives in Minneapolis with her family.

If you enjoyed this book, you'll also want to read
these other Milkweed novels.

To order books or for more information, contact Milkweed
at (800) 520-6455
or visit our Web site (www.milkweed.org).

Border Crossing
Jessica Lee Anderson

Perfect
Natasha Friend

Nissa's Place
A. LaFaye

Beyond the Station Lies the Sea
Jutta Richter

MILKWEED EDITIONS

Founded as a nonprofit organization in 1980, Milkweed Editions is an independent publisher. Our mission is to identify, nurture and publish transformative literature, and build an engaged community around it.

JOIN US

In addition to revenue generated by the sales of books we publish, Milkweed Editions depends on the generosity of institutions and individuals like you. In an increasingly consolidated and bottom-line-driven publishing world, your support allows us to select and publish books on the basis of their literary quality and transformative potential. Please visit our Web site (www.milkweed.org) or contact us at (800) 520-6455 to learn more.

Milkweed Editions, a nonprofit publisher, gratefully acknowledges sustaining support from Maurice and Sally Blanks; Emilie and Henry Buchwald; the Bush Foundation; the Patrick and Aimee Butler Foundation; Timothy and Tara Clark; Betsy and Edward Cussler; the Dougherty Family Foundation; Mary Lee Dayton; Julie B. DuBois; Joanne and John Gordon; Ellen Grace; William and Jeanne Grandy; John and Andrea Gulla; Elizabeth Driscoll Hlavka and Edwin Hlavka; the Jerome Foundation; the Lerner Foundation; the Lindquist & Vennum Foundation; Sanders and Tasha Marvin; Robert E. and Vivian McDonald; the McKnight Foundation; Mid-Continent Engineering; the Minnesota State Arts Board, through an appropriation by the Minnesota State Legislature and a grant from the National Endowment for the Arts; Christine and John L. Morrison; Kelly Morrison and John Willoughby; the National Endowment for the Arts; Ann and Doug Ness; Jörg and Angie Pierach; the RBC Foundation USA; Deborah Reynolds; Cheryl Ryland; Schele and Philip Smith; the Target Foundation; the Travelers Foundation; Moira Turner; and Edward and Jenny Wahl.

Interior design by Ann Sudmeier
Typeset in Weiss
by BookMobile Design and Publishing Services
Printed on acid-free 100% postconsumer waste paper
by Friesens Corporation

ENVIRONMENTAL BENEFITS STATEMENT

Milkweed Editions saved the following resources by printing the pages of this book on chlorine free paper made with 100% post-consumer waste.

TREES	WATER	ENERGY	SOLID WASTE	GREENHOUSE GASES
23	**10,485**	**10**	**665**	**2,325**
FULLY GROWN	GALLONS	MILLION BTUs	POUNDS	POUNDS

Environmental impact estimates were made using the Environmental Paper Network Paper Calculator. For more information visit www.papercalculator.org.